P9-BIJ-892

"Are you trying to get me drunk?" Alex asked.

"Yes."

"That." she told him with a choked giggle. "is a very underhanded and devious thing to do."

"A desperate man will go to desperate lengths." Noah murmured.

"Well. Shakespeare said 'Tempt not a desperate man.' Maybe I'd better go home."

"Stay here and tempt me. Please."

"Noah. if you take advantage of me when I don't know what I'm doing. I shall kill you in the morning."

"Alex. you'll never convince me you don't know exactly what you're doing."

"I can't convince you I'm drunk?"

"Oh. I see." Noah said wickedly. "You were hoping you could beg me to ravish you and then in the morning plead drunken temporary insanity."

"I'd never beg a man to ravish me."

"Then I'll beg. Ravish me. Please."

"Women don't ravish men."

"Set a precedent. Join the distinguished ranks of trailblazers."

Alex looked at him. at the handsome face that was shadowed and highlighted by the fire's glow. and she felt a sudden urge to do some trailblazing. . . .

WHAT ARE *LOVESWEPT* ROMANCES?

They are stories of true romance and touching emotion. We believe those two very important ingredients are constants in our highly sensual and very believable stories in the *LOVESWEPT* line. Our goal is to give you, the reader, stories of consistently high quality that may sometimes make you laugh, sometimes make you cry, but are always fresh and creative and contain many delightful surprises within their pages.

Most romance fans read an enormous number of books. Those they truly love, they keep. Others may be traded with friends and soon forgotten. We hope that each *LOVESWEPT* romance will be a treasure—a "keeper." We will always try to publish

LOVE STORIES YOU'LL NEVER FORGET
BY AUTHORS YOU'LL ALWAYS REMEMBER

The Editors

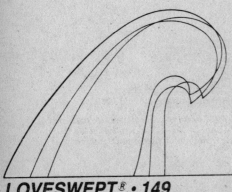

LOVESWEPT® • 149

Kay Hooper
Time After Time

BANTAM BOOKS
TORONTO • NEW YORK • LONDON • SYDNEY • AUCKLAND

TIME AFTER TIME

A Bantam Book / July 1986

LOVESWEPT® and the wave device are registered
trademarks of Bantam Books, Inc. Registered in U.S. Patent
and Trademark Office and elsewhere.

ISBN 0-553-21765-8

Published simultaneously in the United States and Canada

Bantam Books are published by Bantam Books, Inc. Its
trademark, consisting of the words "Bantam Books" and
the portrayal of a rooster, is Registered in U.S. Patent and
Trademark Office and in other countries. Marca Registrada.
Bantam Books, Inc., 666 Fifth Avenue, New York, New
York 10103.

PRINTED IN THE UNITED STATES OF AMERICA

O   0 9 8 7 6 5 4 3 2 1

One

"Miss Cortney-Bennet?"

From some distant corner of the very dark room a tiny, gentle voice reproved him. "It's just Bennet. Most Americans don't use hyphenated names."

A bit rattled for several reasons, he stepped inside the loft and half-closed the door behind him. It was so dark that he had the eerie feeling of having been swallowed up by something huge and dimly threatening. It didn't help that rain lashed the high windows or that thunder rumbled distantly.

"Sorry. Uh—I got a message about a problem."

There was a long silence broken only by a muffled crash as he took an unwary step forward, tripped over something unyielding, and found himself sprawled across what seemed to be a large box. The tiny voice reached him through his muttered curses.

"A slight problem. You may have noticed that it's dark."

"The whole building's dark," he retorted, peeling himself off the box.

"Well, you own the building. Can't you do something about it?" Suspicion abruptly entered the ridiculously small voice. "You do own the building, don't you?"

"Not at all," he responded politely, barking his shin on what felt like a boulder. "I just stopped by to rape and pillage."

"Perfect weather for it," she murmured.

"Look, where *are* you?" he demanded, trying to home in on that small voice.

"I'm not sure. I was in the shower when the lights went out, and I haven't been able to find my flashlight. I just barely found the phone."

Before he could stop himself, he asked, "Did you find any clothes?"

"I found a robe." Her voice turned reflective. "Or maybe it's just the towel Caliban chewed a couple of holes in. It *feels* like a robe, though."

Fascinated, he took a step toward her voice, tripped again, and found himself hugging something tall, unyielding, and furry. Recoiling violently, he tripped going backward and sat down hard on yet another box.

"What the *hell*?"

"I beg your pardon?"

"I just ran into something with fur," he managed to say.

"Is it alive?"

"I sincerely hope not!"

"Oh, well, that was Fluffy. He's a bear. A *stuffed* bear," she added rather hastily.

He took a deep breath. "Oh."

"Yes. Don't you have a flashlight?"

He decided to remain where he was on the box because there was something definitely unnerving in encountering a bear—be it ever so stuffed—in total darkness. "I couldn't find my flashlight," he explained, adding, "I just moved in yesterday myself."

"You're a lot of help," she told him severely. "What *is* your name, anyway? I've forgotten."

"Noah Thorne. And you're Stephanie Alexandra Cortney Bennet," he said, remembering not to hyphenate the surnames. "It stuck in my mind."

"Impressive, isn't it?" she agreed cheerfully. "I was born with it, but use it only professionally. To my friends, I'm just Alex Bennet."

For some time Noah had been conscious of a wry feeling about his mental image of the lady with the impressive name. Now he was certain that image was slightly off. They had never met face to face, or even talked on the phone; he had seen some of her interior decorating and had hired her through correspondence to handle the decorating of his building.

And Alex Bennet, upon learning all the details of the conversion, had instantly requested a loft for herself. She had decided to relocate to San Francisco from the East, and both the job and the loft had sounded perfect to her. But he had been gone all day while she moved in, and they still hadn't met.

Neither of them knew the building at all well—she because it was her first day here, and Noah because he'd been out of town working on a commission while the conversion took place.

It was an old building, a warehouse recently and very roughly converted to lofts. There would be five lofts eventually, although only two were presently habitable: the one he had moved into on the top floor yesterday, and the one Alex Bennet had taken on the first floor today. Neither loft was much more than bare floors and brick walls at this point.

Noah had tired of his apartment in a vast complex downtown, and had instantly decided to move here when the warehouse-conversion idea became feasible. He planned to manage the building himself, taking the top floor as both living and work areas. It would allow him plenty of space and time for his photographic work, he'd decided.

He wondered now if he was being optimistic about having plenty of time. Everything that could go wrong *had* already, and he'd been here only since yesterday. He'd had the plumber out only hours after moving in to fix various clogged drains, requested the building contractor to return in order to close up a doorway somebody had officiously added to the plans, and now it most certainly looked as though the electrician would have to be called.

He sat on a box in a very dark room, wary of moving because of a stuffed bear, and growing more and more curious about his decorator/tenant. He had checked his answering service after leaving his studio late in the afternoon, stopping by a phone booth because his home phone hadn't been connected yet, and his studio phone had just been disconnected since it was his last day in the place.

There was little he could do about the situation, but when his service reported a problem with his tenant, he'd felt honor-bound at least to find out what the problem was. Encountering darkness upon entering the building, he'd felt his way cautiously up the three flights of stairs to his own loft, searched fruitlessly for a flashlight, then felt his way back down the stairs to Alex's loft.

For all the good it had done either of them.

Suddenly aware of the silence, he suggested, "Matches? Candles?"

"Are you kidding? I couldn't even find my clothes."

Noah calculated the position of the bear, carefully got off his box-chair, and made another attempt to work his way toward her voice. When his outstretched fingers encountered fur, he jerked his hand back, silently damned his sense of direction, made a ten-degree correction, and went on.

The next few minutes were strange, to say the least. Locating a wall by nearly running headlong into it, he felt along it until he found a door. Opening the door was an instinctive reaction—and so was hastily shutting it when a deep and eerily menacing growl issued from within.

"What in heaven's name—?"

"That's just Caliban. You said I could have a pet," she reminded him anxiously. "He's very well-trained."

Noah decided not to ask exactly what kind of pet Caliban was; judging by the sound of his growl, he was a big one. Making another guess as to the location of his tenant, he turned and tentatively started back across the room. "It would be much simpler," he said, "if we just went out and got flashlights and oil lamps."

"Well, I hate to be a bother," she told him, "but *you'll* have to do that. I'm not dressed to go anywhere. At least I don't think I am. Won't the power come back on?"

"If lightning hit a transformer or something," he replied, "and work crews are out. But if it's just this building, who knows when we'll have power?"

"I called the power company; they said it was the storm."

"Did they estimate when service might be restored?"

"Apparently they didn't dare. I called your service again to let you know what they said, but you'd already checked in for the last time. I really didn't think there was anything you could do, but . . ." Her voice trailed off for a moment, then resumed rather stolidly. "But I've never been totally alone in a strange city before—with no lights—and I got a little nervous."

Instantly he said, "I don't blame you. A strange

apartment is bad enough, but in the dark? My heart's still pounding from running into your bear."

She giggled, and since the voice sounded very near, Noah reached out an experimental hand. "Is that—"

"Yes, that's me," she said, startled and slightly breathless.

He swiftly drew back his hand. "Um . . . sorry." She had a little-girl voice, he reflected, but there was nothing childish about what his hand had encountered.

Alex cleared her throat. "Blind man's buff has its pitfalls. Look, I'm near the couch. I'll back up and move sideways, and if you take a step forward, I think we can both sit down."

Gingerly they managed the feat.

"I really should go out and find some kind of light," he said, "but, quite frankly, I'm not looking forward to making my way back to the door."

"That's why I stayed in one place," she confided. "Since the loft is basically one huge room, with only a bedroom and bath separate from it, the movers pretty much just dumped everything and left. I think Caliban was making them nervous."

Something about that name bothered Noah, but he couldn't pin it down; he only knew that every mention of the name twanged a cord of uneasy memory. "He isn't vicious, is he?"

"Oh, no. He's just big. And he looks a bit . . . um . . . unusual." Before Noah could comment, she was going on cheerfully, "I must say, I've never before met a client under circumstances like these. Or a landlord, for that matter. Are you going to be a good land-lord?"

Both taken aback and amused by the question, he answered gravely. "I certainly hope so. But I'm new at it, so you'll have to bear with me—no pun intended."

She giggled, a curiously enchanting, gleeful sound, and Noah felt his interest in her growing. She *couldn't* be as young as she sounded, although if his encounter with womanly curves was anything to go by, she was certainly much shorter than the average woman. He decided that there was something vastly intriguing about this meeting. It was, he knew, because of the total darkness; with sight no help to him, he found himself using other senses more intensely than he could ever remember doing before.

His ears found the sound of her voice pleasant and musical, the very small and low-pitched timbre of it oddly fascinating. She smelled of herbal soap, reminding him of a dark-green forest after a spring shower. And though they were not touching, he could feel the warmth of her beside him on the couch. Questions filled his mind, and in the enigmatic darkness those questions were a tantalizing mystery.

Upon hearing the name Stephanie Alexandra Cortney Bennet, Noah had fleetingly visualized a tall and queenly woman, chic, sophisticated, and with a strong sense of style. Alex was a free-lance decorator, which meant either that she was very successful, hadn't been at it very long, or else was taking a tre-mendous gamble on her own abilities. He knew of two apartment buildings she'd done in the East—the work he'd seen and been impressed by—and both clients had spoken well of her.

Now that he thought about it, both those clients had also seemed a bit bemused, and the remarks, identical from both men, now rose in his memory. "*She's a very good decorator.*" Not an unexpected remark from a satisfied customer, to be sure, Noah thought. But . . . somehow peculiar.

Unconsciously he began listening even more intently with every sense, both curiosity and a pleasurable feeling of mystery prodding him. And something else, some odd, compelling sense of . . . certainty? "Did you just get into town today?" he asked, wanting to hear more of her oddly fascinating little voice.

"Yes, this morning. It was a long drive."

"You drove?" he exclaimed. "Across the country?"

"The pioneers blazed a trail," she reminded him, amused. "I just followed it."

"But you didn't drive alone?"

"Except for Caliban. It was fun, really. I got to see a lot of the country, and whenever I needed to rest, I just pulled over somewhere and slept in the van."

In spite of darkness, reality was taking an even sharper turn away from his imaginings: She was obviously not the chic, first-class traveler he'd expected.

"So you just literally pulled up roots and came out here? What about your family?"

"Don't have one. My parents were killed when I was six, and there weren't any close relatives. I was raised in an orphanage."

"That's tough," he said, his ready sympathy stirred.

"Oh, no, not at all." Alex was cheerful. "It was a nice place operated by good people. I left about ten years ago, just after I turned sixteen. I didn't run *away* from there as much as I ran *to* something else."

"What did you run to?" he asked, curious.

"The circus."

"What?"

She chuckled. "The orphanage took us to see the circus about a year before I left, and it kind of, well, obsessed me. So I decided to run away and join the circus."

"And that's what you did?"

"Certainly. It was a plan."

"A plan?"

"I like to plan things. So I waited until another circus passed through town, and when they left, I left with them."

"No one tried to send you back?"

"I lied about my age. Besides, I was good with animals and they needed a trainer. It wasn't a very big circus," she added ruefully.

"So you became their animal trainer."

"That's right. I trained whatever they asked me to train. Primates, elephants, dogs, horses, cats."

"Cats?"

"The big cats."

"Don't tell me you put your head in a lion's mouth?"

"You'd be surprised," she murmured.

Noah was more than a little incredulous. "How on earth did an animal trainer wind up being an interior decorator?"

"Growth."

"I beg your pardon?"

"Growth. I believe that people have to change constantly in order to grow as human beings. I left the circus after about four years because it was time for me to change, to do something else."

"And what did you do?" he asked, fascinated.

"Well, several things. I left the circus in Richmond and ran into an old friend from the orphange; she had a business and asked me to join her, so I did. I got my high school diploma and took some college courses while I was there. When she decided to move her business—it was an arts and crafts place—I just stayed on in Richmond. After that I did different things. I worked in a bank, and a realty company, and a museum. Then I took courses in decorating, and decided to try that for a while."

The thumbnail sketch told him more, probably, than she'd intended. It told him she was versatile, strong-minded, and very self-reliant. She had spent ten years settled in an orphanage, then four years traveling the Gypsy circuit of circus performers before settling again in the East.

Though he couldn't help but believe that her life in the orphanage had been a bland one, she had more than made up for that during the past few years. And he had an odd but strong feeling that if she had gone into detail, he would have found even more fascinating enigmas.

At that moment Noah's strongest desire was for a single match. Though lightning had flashed intermittently, the high glazed windows of the loft permitted little light to penetrate—and none at all long enough for them even to glimpse each other.

And he very badly wanted to see her.

"My kingdom for a match," he muttered, unaware of speaking aloud.

Alex clearly sensed nothing personal in the remark. "It is dark, isn't it? I've never seen dark like this before. Why on earth did you leave the windows so high?"

"I didn't want to change the basic structure of the building," he answered automatically. "Will it present problems for decorating?"

"I doubt it: lofts look better without drapes anyway. But if you don't have the power company put a couple of streetlights nearby, your other tenants might complain."

Amused at the critical advice, he murmured, "The power company's coming out next week: there'll be two utility lights out front and one in back. I'll have floodlights around the pool too."

"There's a pool?" she asked eagerly.

"Just finished. It isn't huge, but since this building is miles away from a health club, I thought a pool would be pleasant and convenient."

"And there's quite a bit of cleared land around this building, isn't there?" Alex sounded thoughtful.

"A couple of acres, and fenced. It seemed like a good investment: I can always have more buildings constructed later if I decide to go that way. Apartments and lofts are at a real premium around here."

"So this is an investment for you?"

"More or less."

"You mentioned in your letter that you're a photographer, and that part of your loft will be a studio. Have you decided whether or not I'm to decorate your loft as well as the others?"

"After seeing how bare everything is—definitely. If it suits you, we'll take care of our lofts first, then you can work on the other three."

"Fine."

While the conversation had progressed casually, a part of Noah's mind had been idly considering why he had fumbled his way across a dark room just to be near her. He remembered reading of various city-wide blackouts during which people had tended to stick together and form quick friendships—most of which had instantly dissolved when the lights came back on. Was that it? A very human tendency to find companionship in order to ward off the inherent danger of darkness? Rather the way cavemen must have huddled together around a fire with deadly wilderness at their backs . . .

There was something about total darkness that stripped away the caution most people felt upon encountering strangers. Unable to see, there was no need to guard expressions or to wonder worriedly if dinner had left a stain on an otherwise clean shirt.

There was only darkness that seemed to intensify each sound, each shift in movement.

Noah wondered if his own fascination would dissolve when the lights came back on, wondered if Alex Bennet would be nearly as interesting when he could see her.

And then his questions were answered.

Two

When his eyes had stopped squinting from the sudden light. Noah found that Alex had recovered her own vision with the quickness of a cat. She was looking at him. wide-eyed. and her obvious surprise gave him a few moments to try to cope with his own.

For an instant he felt a hazy yet jarring sense of déjà vu. Another face flashed across his mind. But the memory fled before he could know anything except that it was not this face. The eyes were the same. though. the enchanting green eyes. Or perhaps the soul behind them . . .

A violent mental shove sent the unnerving idea spinning away. and Noah forced himself to think only of this face and this woman. It was not. in the end. very hard to do.

Stephanie Alexandra Cortney Bennet was a woman

tiny enough to match her voice; she might have been five feet tall on her very best day and wearing three-inch heels. She had on a white robe that looked more like a scanty beach coverup, the lapels barely covering curves that were startlingly generous for so petite a woman, the hem only just reaching the middle of her thighs. She was tanned a golden brown over every inch of exposed flesh.

And she possessed the kind of delicate, fragile beauty that would always turn heads and stop conversations in mid-sentence. Blond curls, thick and with the texture of spun silk, tumbled to her shoulders, framing a face that was right out of a dream. It was an oval face, golden and flawless. Delicate brows winged above large, expressive eyes of such a clear green that Noah half-expected to see a siren beckon to him from their depths; dark lashes tangled in a long, curling thicket that was a sooty frame for the green. Her nose was finely etched and straight, her mouth gently curved with humor and vulnerability.

Noah caught himself leaning instinctively toward her, and felt a jarring shock. There *were* sirens in her eyes, he thought dimly, innocent sirens beckoning with guileless smiles and the timeless grace of ancient seas. Then she spoke, and although the sirens continued to exist in green depths, now they laughed like forest sprites. . . .

"I thought you'd be short, fat, and balding!"

"Thanks," he shot back, conscious of the huskiness in his own voice.

"Sorry, Noah, but I was going by past experience;

all the photographers I've known have looked like that."

Trying to distract himself from the sirens, Noah tore his gaze away to look around the room, and he succeeded very well when he saw Fluffy. "Good Lord!"

Incredibly the stuffed bear was of the polar variety, standing very tall and wearing a fierce grimace of bearlike rage. Noah marveled fleetingly that the stark white had been so invisible in the darkness, realizing that the room had been even darker than he'd thought. His gaze flitted over the confusion of boxes, crates, and furniture, absently noting that the "boulder" he'd barked his shin on was in actuality a large crate that lay open and empty except for a pile of clean straw.

Straw? he thought. *Now, why on earth—*

"It's nice to meet you," Alex said solemnly, holding out one small hand.

"Same here." Holding that soft slenderness in his own hand, Noah found it impossible to believe—"Are you sure you tamed lions?" he blurted out.

"Very sure." Her amused smile made it quite obvious that she'd heard that question before.

Noah found himself wondering if the sirens in her eyes had bewitched even jungle beasts, and hastily pushed the speculation away. He also released her hand when he became aware that he'd held it longer than necessary. He felt rattled again and wasn't at all sure he liked the sensation. Alex didn't seem to notice.

She rose to her feet, smiling. "Let me get changed

and I'll put on some coffee. Unless—?" Her lifted brow made the question clear.

"I'd love some coffee, thanks," he responded. As he watched her move gracefully through the jumble toward the bathroom, Noah told himself that his desire to remain was simply a landlord's intention to get to know a tenant, and a client's desire to better know his decorator. He told himself that several times, more firmly with each repetition.

And he believed not one word of it.

By the time he made his way up the stairs to his own loft over an hour later, Noah had stopped pretending even to himself. Alex Bennet was the most captivating woman he'd ever met in his life, and even after seeing the polar bear she clearly meant to keep in her own loft, he felt no misgivings about her decorating ability; she could have done every loft in the building in bamboo and stuffed wildlife and he wouldn't have said a word against it.

He'd even given Fluffy an absent pat on his way out.

It wasn't until much later, sliding between the sheets of his bed and reaching to turn out the lamp, that Noah wondered about Caliban. Alex had not suggested that he meet her pet, and he had been too intrigued by the woman herself to care about anything else. Now he wondered, but only fleetingly. He lay back and closed his eyes, looking forward to tomorrow.

He dreamed of mermaids and sirens, his dreamself incredulous that Ulysses had lashed himself to a mast instead of leaping happily overboard. . . .

Noah woke once in the night, and during the hazy moments between abandoned dreams and wakefulness, he could have sworn he heard a voice. The voice was feminine, familiar yet strange, and the accent was one he'd never heard before. And his sleep-fogged mind told him the girl spoke to him—but to someone else as well.

"Oh, see! Our lifelines match! We are bonded, my love. Fated to share all our lives together!"

And then he was awake.

Noah frowned into the darkness, feeling an oddly displaced sensation. Green woods, he thought, not a dark bedroom . . . Then he shook his head, pounded his pillow, and fought to recapture sleep.

But he never recaptured the dream.

Alex puttered about her loft for a while after Noah left. She let Caliban out of the bedroom and fed him, reminding herself to be sure to go shopping early the next day. It was late, the storm long gone, and she waited restlessly for her pet to finish his dinner so that she could take him out for his much-needed exercise.

Absently unpacking a box filled with decorative pillows, she piled them on the couch and then sat down among them, finally thinking about what she'd been trying to avoid considering. There were several things, and heading the list was her new client and landlord.

The return of electricity had brought a definite

shock, one she still hadn't entirely recovered from. Her supposedly short-fat-and-balding client was no such thing; in fact, any comparison with that mythical gentleman was ludicrous.

Noah Thorne was a man somewhere in his mid-thirties, somewhere over six feet tall, and somewhere over a ten in the half-serious rating system Alex's friends always used.

Alex had never even met a ten before, much less a man who would easily jolt the needle over the top.

He had the kind of hawklike good looks one never expected to encounter in a real person, and if that smile hadn't been breaking hearts for a good many years, she mused, then Noah Thorne had met a lot of blind women. His thick hair was raven-black and stick-straight, his eyes a curious light blue that was almost gray and almost silver—but not quite.

Half the women Alex knew would have killed to possess his long eyelashes, and the other half would have killed to possess *him.* After seeing him move around the loft, Alex had been reminded irresistibly of a warrior walking cat-footed on the hunt, silent, dangerous, and nearly as wild as the game he stalked.

When he smiled, that lethal image was overshadowed by charm and humor, but Alex felt faintly unnerved by the instinct telling her that nature had intended just that; even the wildest of beasts could look cuddly and unthreatening at times, lending a feeling of safety that was, to say the least, misleading.

Alex was determined not to be misled.

However, it was one thing for her to tell herself

that, and quite another thing to ignore the instant attraction she'd felt. She'd seen the ridiculous images in her mind of Cleopatra meeting Antony, of Guinevere gazing upon Lancelot, of Cinderella raising her eyes to meet those of Prince Charming. . . .

Ridiculous! She was twenty-six years old, on her own for ten years, and she certainly knew better than to indulge in childish dreams and unrealistic expectations. Men were men; the best of them possessed annoying habits and beliefs, and the worst of them had some redeeming trait. Period.

Still, there was just something *about* the man. She'd had the odd feeling that they had met before, yet his face had struck no cord of memory.

Alex drummed her fingers silently on a particularly colorful pillow and tried to think reasonably. He was a very attractive man, and in the moment of surprise following the darkness she had seen his interest in her. He had drunk her coffee and gazed at her almost constantly, making her feel breathless and curiously unlike herself—and that was a danger signal.

In fact, it was a hell of a potential problem.

Because Alex wanted very much to get to know him better. It wasn't his looks that prompted that desire, although they had certainly been a jolt to her system. No, she thought, it wasn't because he was a handsome man. It was because of the humor in his deep voice and the charm and danger of his smile.

Danger. Alex knew then why she was so attracted to him. For nearly four years, while most girls her age had been playfully experimenting with boys, Alex had learned to handle creatures of the wild. She had learned to read the signs of rage in the posture of a big cat, in the abrupt movement of a bear, and in the flashing eyes of a stallion. And she had survived those years and experiences unscathed because she was very good at reading such signs.

Smiling a little to herself, Alex allowed that instinct to search her impressions of tonight's meeting with Noah, and her instinct summed up the situation neatly. *A caged lion, a tethered hawk, a chained bear . . . call him what you will, Noah Thorne is a dangerous man.*

Not dangerous to life and limb, of course, but dangerous to something far more vital. Alex had the strong feeling that any involvement with Noah would literally change her life forever.

So what? You approve of change, a voice in her head pointed out reasonably.

So there was a problem. Caliban.

Alex looked up as he padded silently around the low partition dividing the kitchen from the rest of the loft, and rose to her feet. "Ready to go out, boy?" Caliban rumbled something that might have been a yes, his big yellow eyes gazing at her with a gentleness she could read and no one else would ever believe.

"Now, look," she told him, scrabbling through a box for his collar and leash, "we can't let anyone know you're here. So you behave yourself, all right?" After nearly six years of successfully hiding her pet, Alex normally would have had little fear of exposure. Except that now she'd met Noah.

Whether he would keep her secret or not she didn't know, but both her job and her interest in him promised a closer involvement than she'd ever had to deal with during the past six years. Noah had her definite interest, but Caliban had her heart—and sooner than lose him, she knew she would quietly fold her tent and steal away into the night.

Sighing, wondering how long she could keep Caliban's presence a secret from her landlord—to say nothing of future tenants—Alex fastened the heavy collar around his thick neck and snapped the leash in place. Then, while he waited patiently, she went through the routine of finding out whether or not there was anyone in the vicinity outside the building.

Feeling fortunate to have a ground-floor loft with a back entrance, Alex checked the rear of the building and felt even luckier. The pool was to the right of her back door, new wooden decking surrounding it and a decorative fence surrounding that; the gate stood open, giving her a good look inside since the moon now shone in a cloudless sky.

Directly outside the sliding glass door was an equally new deck matched by another several yards away for the other ground-floor loft. Looking up, she could see that each loft boasted a deck with a view of the pool. Alex sighed, hoping that neither Noah nor any of the future tenants would spend late nights out on their decks. Then she gazed at the fenced land surrounding this building.

For what was basically a city dwelling, she thought, there was an abundance of empty land, which was

just great for her purposes. She stepped out far
enough to look up toward Noah's loft, assuring herself that it was dark and that he wasn't on his deck.
He might well have been inside in darkness, gazing
through his own glass door, but she doubted it.

Ten minutes later she and Caliban were exploring,
and she was patiently teaching her pet where his
boundaries were. They roamed among the dripping
trees and wet, overgrown grass for more than an hour
before she finally led him back inside the loft and got
ready for bed.

Later, lying sleepily in the darkness of her bedroom, she automatically moved over as Caliban
climbed into the bed. She patted his broad head and
listened to the grumbling sound he made in contentment. Just as she was dropping off to sleep, she
found herself wondering idly how her pet would react
to a man in her bed.

Odd . . . the question had never occurred to her
before.

She had taken Caliban out for a run at dawn, then
accomplished her shopping before most of the city
was even awake; all-night grocery stores, she thought
with amusement, were certainly a godsend for people
with unusual pets. So was the ability to sleep no more
than four or five hours a night, an ability she had
possessed as long as she could remember.

Leaving Caliban in the bedroom to sleep off the
morning's exertions and his breakfast, she put away

her groceries and began to get her kitchen in order while she watched the sun rising outside. Several hours later she fixed a late breakfast for herself and gazed in approval at her new home. The kitchen was in order and her living area arranged neatly, a profusion of pillows piled on her long sectional couch and two overstuffed chairs. Several large decorative candles graced her inlaid oak coffee table—she'd never again be caught here in the dark for long!—and ceramic and porcelain lamps sat on the end tables that matched it.

Fluffy stood in a corner near the door with two large potted rubber plants flanking him. Alex had efficiently and as quietly as possible erected her sectional bookcases along the broad wall on the other side of the door, and small boxes of books stood ready to be put into place.

She had taken apart Caliban's crate and stored the panels in the capacious closet between the bedroom and bathroom doors before stuffing the straw into a large garbage bag along with other assorted trash familiar to anyone who had ever moved. Empty boxes were piled neatly near the door awaiting removal.

It was a good start.

Moving about the loft, thoughtful, Alex carried her coffee cup and planned. The raised platform that took up half the open loft space and ran the length of the streetside wall, she decided, would hold her working materials. It already did, in fact, since she'd asked the movers to leave her working table, desk, and various tools of her trade up there. A wide set of three steps led up to the platform, and Caliban sprawled to block the way.

Amused, she watched as he methodically licked the bedraggled face of the large teddy bear he clutched between his front paws. "I'm glad the doll finally disintegrated," she told him, smiling. "That bear's bad enough, but the doll made your instincts look suspect." He blinked sleepy eyes and began washing the bear's face again.

Remembering the large doll her pet had dragged around for nearly two years, Alex smiled. But then a knock sounded at her door, and her smile vanished. "Cal!" she hissed, heading for the bedroom door.

He got up and lifted the bear in his huge jaws, obediently following her and going into the bedroom. She watched him climb onto her bed with his toy, then carefully closed the door and went to find out who her visitor was.

Noah.

He stepped into the loft with a cheerful smile, saying, "Good morning, Alex. I thought you could probably use some help—" Then his eyes widened as he took in the neatly arranged living area of the loft. "You're a fast worker, aren't you?" he observed, surprised.

"An early riser." Alex smiled as she closed the door behind him. "I'll have it to do all over again, probably, when the painters come, but I wanted to get an idea of how it'll look. Coffee?"

"Thanks." He followed her into the kitchen area, his eyes drawn irresistibly to the lovely picture she made dressed in snug jeans and a colorful peasant blouse. A bright bandanna held her thick hair away from her face, making her look even more fragile than she had the night before. And the sirens, he decided, were still present in her eyes, but this morning they were wistful creatures with gentle smiles.

Bewitched. He was definitely bewitched, and he wondered distantly why that didn't disturb him.

"Do all the lofts have the same floor plan?" she asked him, handing over a cup of coffee.

He nodded. "Except mine, which basically has double the space."

Her green eyes were bright as she looked around her own loft. "Possibilities. Definite possibilities."

They had moved back into the living area, and he laughed as he looked at the profusion of pillows. "I've never seen so many before," he replied to her inquiring look. "D'you collect them?"

"No, I throw them," she answered casually.

Noah sat down on the couch at her gesture, watching her get comfortable a foot or so away and wondering if he'd missed a turn somewhere in the conversation. "You throw them?"

"Uh-huh."

"Why?" he asked blankly.

"It's better than breaking things, isn't it?"

He took a sip of his coffee. "You've lost me."

She smiled suddenly, and the sirens became mischievous sprites. "I have a terrible temper, and when I'm mad, I have to *do* something. I broke an awful lot of things before I discovered the pillows: they satisfy my urge to throw things, but nothing breaks."

Noah became conscious of a sudden desire to watch her get mad. It was a totally unreasonable urge, and he didn't want to *make* her mad: he just wanted to see her throw pillows. He fought the urge.

"Oh. Um . . . you just throw the pillows?"

"And yell," she added happily.

Imagining that tiny voice roused to a yell was almost more than his mind could grasp: it seemed an impossible thing. Both the yelling and the pillow-throwing, in fact, seemed impossible, given her tiny, fragile appearance.

Clearly Alex saw his disbelief. "It's true," she assured him. "I used to have the most famous temper tantrums in the orphanage, and even now my friends hide behind things when I get mad."

"Should I take that example to heart?"

She smiled, but there was something about the smile implying a definite warning. "You'd better."

"I'm not planning to make you mad," he told her.

"Best-laid plans, and all that. *Something* is bound to make me mad sooner or later."

Noah thought about that for a moment, flipped a mental coin, and didn't even bother to see how it landed. "Do amorous photographers make you mad?" he asked gravely.

Alex sipped her coffee, and the sirens in her eyes seemed to laugh at him. "Noah," she asked dryly, "are you making a pass?"

"I planned to be more subtle than that," he told her, pained.

Her eyes were definitely laughing. "Oh. Well, to answer your question—as I said before, all the photographers I've known have been short, fat, and so on. Fatherly in fact. I've never met an amorous photographer, so I don't know how I'd react."

"Best guess?"

She reflected. "Best guess—I doubt it. On principle, you understand. Of course, there's no saying for sure. The amorous photographer in question could easily do or say something to set me off."

"For instance?"

"Oh, any little thing could do it. The wrong word or gesture. A frown instead of a smile. Who can say?"

"Then you'd throw pillows."

"And yell."

He nodded, still grave. "Any jealous suitors hanging around likely to cause trouble?"

"You mean you wouldn't be willing to fight for me?" she asked, wounded.

"How could I impress a lion tamer with my fighting ability?" he asked, a suitably rueful expression on his handsome face. "I'm defeated before I start. And answer the question, please."

"Suitors? There weren't any the last time I looked."

"Maybe they couldn't compete with a lion tamer either."

She giggled suddenly. "I never noticed anyone trying. You've got lion tamers on the brain, Noah. It was quite a few years ago, you know, and I rarely pick up a whip and chair to demonstrate my skills. How about you? Any ladies lurking about?"

"Not recently," he told her, deadpan.

"That's good. I'd better warn you that I never stand in line for anything but the movies. One of my little quirks, I'm afraid."

"Jealousy?"

Instantly she shook her head. "No, that isn't it. Life's too short to take second place to anything. If I get involved with a man, it has to be a blue-ribbon affair, or it won't be any more than a beginning."

"If you get involved." He was watching her intently now, surprise in his blue eyes. "You haven't, have you?"

She looked at him for a moment, then shook her head with a faint smile. "I haven't. Nobody waved a blue ribbon." Abruptly sober, she added, "A few of my friends used to call me a vanishing breed, but they stopped laughing after a while. They'd wake up in the morning to an empty bed and a note on the pillow after one of their casual 'encounters,' and the night before didn't seem as enjoyable as it had at the time."

Noah gazed at her silently as he absorbed her meaning. It wasn't that her standards were too high, he realized. Not *who* but *how*. She carried no dream of Prince Charming, no image of physical perfection; all she asked—demanded—was the kind of committed caring that most people realized their need for only after much trial and error. And her next quiet words confirmed his thoughts.

"I'm not looking for a ring and a promise, but it has

to be more than just the moment. It has to be important. So I'd warn the . . . amorous photographer . . . that I'm still looking for that blue ribbon, and I won't settle for less."

He smiled slightly. "Will you know it when you find it?"

"Yes." The one word, calm and simple. She would know.

Noah shook his head. "You're an unusual woman, Alex."

"Not at all. Just between you and me, that little spiel of mine has scared off a few would-be suitors."

Noah wasn't deceived by the flippant comment, but he could see that she was growing uncomfortable with the light, humorous flirtation that had become too serious. Besides, he knew only too well that they were still virtual strangers, and a part of him was wary of instant attraction.

They had time.

Alex was astonished at herself. Why on earth, she wondered, had she taken the opportunity of Noah's teasing to offer a very serious warning? Oh, she knew that he had been more than half serious himself, knew that he'd cloaked definite interest in light words. So why had she turned the tables on him? Instead of remaining in the well-defined role of possibilities-should-be-lightly-explored, Alex had instantly stepped out of her part to deliver the warning generally presented much later.

According to her rulebook of new relationships—her own private experience of how relationships tended to progress—first came the light probing she and Noah had ventured into. Next came a different and more serious kind of probing along the lines of likes and dislikes and similarities between the two. Somewhere during these two steps, Alex had found, either attraction or disinterest developed with the inevitable physical closeness or a parting of the ways. That was where she'd always given her warning.

Beyond that point, she'd never gone.

Alex knew that men were attracted to her—past experience told her that quite plainly—but she was quite aware that she was either too demanding or else was less attractive on closer association. It had caused her no heartbreak in the past because she herself had never been interested enough in a man to care when he either became a friend or else faded into the misty night.

During the past years men had told her in tones varying from bewilderment to desperation that she was an unusual woman. She had never been sure precisely what that meant, and no one had offered to enlighten her. Noah had made the comment, and she wondered what he meant by it.

Unusual? Like dodos and dinosaurs, a relic of a bygone age?

Alex didn't know, and didn't plan to ask him. She was too concerned with her own skipping of steps, too bothered by a warning that had come too soon.

And an attraction that had come too soon. She had

felt it instantly, first a strong curiosity about a stranger's face in the darkness and then breathless surprise when that face had been revealed to her. After seeing that face, surprise at her own attraction had faded. *Of course* she was attracted to the man; she'd have to be blind or made of stone not to be.

So why had she warned him? Because past experience told her that interest always faded within a short time? Or had she warned him because her own intense attraction to him frightened her? Because she knew that Noah could be the most important man in her life—or hurt her terribly?

Alex had faced lions without fear. She had helped to tranquilize a bull elephant run amok. She had more than once waded into a group of angry tigers to separate them.

But when she thought of Noah Thorne, of hawklike good looks, a silent, Indian-file walk, and a smile that was charm and danger, Alex felt a sudden urge to pick up a whip and chair.

Three

___

The next few days hardly bore out her misgivings. She and Noah were very occupied, each in settling into new homes and both in discussions and plans about decorating those homes. Noah was casually friendly and companionable, but no more, and Alex was grateful for that.

She was grateful for that primarily because she was having a very difficult time as it was in keeping Caliban hidden from her landlord; if she'd had to deal with romantic interludes as well, she would have gone quietly crazy. Luckily her pet slept long hours during the day, and was perfectly content to remain shut up in her bedroom . . . usually.

In the past, Caliban had always shown only disinterest in people other than Alex. Perfectly friendly in a face-to-face encounter, he never sought out other people.

Until now. To Alex's intense frustration and worry, it seemed that Caliban was curious about the only other occupant of the building. Coming down from Noah's loft late the second day to find some material swatches, she encountered Caliban on the stairs and hastily led him back into her own loft. A moment's inspection showed her that the bedroom door had a tricky latch, and that she had apparently failed to secure the front door; there were no claw marks, no indication that her pet had forced either door.

At that moment Noah called down the stairs to ask if she needed help in finding the swatches, and Caliban, attracted by the voice, started back toward the front door. Alex had a hell of a time wrestling the four hundred pounds of her pet back into the bedroom.

And that was only the second day.

Half a dozen times during the next week Caliban remained a secret only by the skin of Alex's teeth. For six years an exceptionally obedient pet, he now seemed determined to get both himself and his owner in a great deal of trouble. Escaping Alex outside late one night, he dashed through the open gate and gave a roaming German shepherd a near heart attack. The next day he apparently discovered—for the first time in his life—that he had claws, and proceeded to sharpen them on trees outside and doorjambs inside; it took some frantic work with sandpaper and putty by Alex to hide the long gouges he made on the bedroom doorjamb, and she could only cross her fingers and hope no one noticed scars on the trees outside.

A water-loving oddity of his kind, Caliban discovered the pool on the fourth day and thereafter demanded a swim every morning. And when painters and paperhangers began their work, they had to be reassured by Alex that the eerie moaning they heard came from a harmless pet.

Noah seemed to notice nothing unusual, or at least that's what Alex thought. Until midway through the second week.

The painters in Noah's loft made staying there uncomfortable, and Alex had reached the point of strictly avoiding his presence in her own loft. It was an unusually hot and sunny day, and since the pool offered coolness, she suggested they take advantage of it. She regretted the suggestion, however, when Noah took the opportunity to voice his puzzlement.

"I heard the oddest noise last night," he told her, floating lazily on his back.

"Really?" Alex managed to say after treading water fiercely long enough to stop the coughing brought on by swallowing a mouthful of water.

"Yeah. Howling—no, moaning. Gave me the strangest urge to look over my shoulder. Africa."

"Africa?" she queried faintly.

Noah, his eyes closed against the sun's brightness, looked thoughtful. "Well, it made me think of Africa. Those movies you see with all the weird animal noises, I guess."

"Oh." Alex began to methodically swim laps. She

stopped after a lap and a half for two reasons: Because it occurred to her that if Caliban heard splashes, he might decide to join them, and because Noah changed the subject.

Or did he?

"When do I get to meet Caliban?" he asked abruptly.

Alex saw both her new job and her new home disappear in front of her eyes. "Oh, I don't know," she answered vaguely.

"Does his name fit him?"

"His name?"

Noah shifted position, no longer floating but treading water to face her. "If I remember correctly," he said, "Caliban is a character in Shakespeare's *Tempest*. A savage, deformed slave, I think."

"Not my Caliban," she said lightly. "Besides, I didn't name him." She tried to decipher the expression Noah wore, realizing that it was something akin to determination.

"Alex," Noah said very gently, "is there something you aren't telling me about your pet? A special something, I mean?"

Staring into the compelling blue of his eyes, Alex knew a fleeting sensation of panic. Not for Caliban, but for herself. The secret of "taming" wild animals was twofold: first, convincing the creature to accept a trainer as one of its own kind, and then, to persuade that creature—through the skillful art of bluff—that the trainer is superior, dominant.

Gazing into Noah's eyes, Alex recalled the peculiar

image of how the big cats had so often looked at her in submission—but this time she was gazing through the cat's eyes at Noah. And he wasn't bluffing.

What she had only sensed intuitively before now hit her with the force of a blow. She was attracted to Noah because of the element of danger she sensed in him, and that frightened her because she now recognized a strength greater than any she had faced before.

In the circus there had been a very old trainer who had taught Alex the skills she had needed, and she suddenly remembered a pet theory of his. He believed that only "alpha" or dominant personalities ever became successful trainers. Because, he said, only those innately strong people could convince a savage creature to bend its proud neck. He had said that Alex was an alpha person, a rarity among women.

And he had predicted lightly, casually, that it would be difficult for her to find a man she could "run in harness" with. Only an equally strong alpha could match her, he'd said, and they were uncommon indeed. She would, he'd said confidently, know when she met one.

She knew.

There was no need of some feat of strength from Noah, no need of the beating of chest or shouting of power. What she saw in his eyes was a quiet, understated strength, but beneath that was a flaring of something sharp-edged and primitive. It was as if the strongest cat she had ever faced looked at her now with blue-gray eyes.

And Alex felt an equally primitive flaring within her. It was not in her to submit, and her clamoring instincts were telling her now that she was in danger of doing just that. He was stronger. Somehow, he was stronger, and she knew now that his casual companionship of the past days had been the deadly patient waiting of a wild thing.

"Alex?"

She blinked, looking at him, seeing how deceptively civilization could cloak in gentle colors the heart and spirit of a wild thing. She had forgotten his question, and when a shout reached them from Noah's balcony, relief swept over her.

"Alex!" one of the painters yelled. "We need you up here!"

She stroked quickly to the ladder and pulled herself up, mumbling something that might have been an "Excuse me" as she reached for her lavender cotton coverup and donned it without bothering to towel off.

Noah watched her disappear through her sliding glass doors, then pulled himself from the water and sank down on a recently purchased lounge chair to stare broodingly into the sparkling water of the pool.

Since he had taken a few weeks vacation to settle into his new home and set up his studio, there had been far too much time for thinking. Noah would have preferred to be busy, devoting only part of his time to coming to terms with the fascination he felt for Alex.

She was a puzzle, and he had always enjoyed delving to the heart of any mystery.

He had watched her unobtrusively these last days, his photographer's eye catching unguarded moments when he had yearned for a camera in his hand. Like the moment when she had stood in a group of large, coveralled painters, dwarfed by their size yet curiously dominant because all heads had been bent attentively to hers. And the moment coming down the stairs from his loft when she had suddenly thrown a leg across the railing and slid gleefully downward, the green sprites in her eyes laughing up at him.

And other moments. Pensive moments, humorous moments. Moments of frowning concentration and moments of odd, elusive wistfulness.

She seemed a dozen women in a single lovely skin, and she haunted more than his dreams. After her deliberate warning Noah had carefully backed off and settled down to wait, something in him certain that the time would be well spent.

Yet she had looked at him just now with a startling intensity, as if she had rounded a corner to face a threat looming in front of her. He had forgotten his own question as he'd gazed into green eyes flaring with turbulent emotion and felt something in himself stir to wakefulness.

Now he was restless, on edge. What had he said to provoke that reaction in her? He'd asked about Caliban. Just that. In fleeting moments during the past days he had wondered idly about Alex's pet, still faintly bothered by the name. Then he had traced the memory to Shakespeare, and had still been only mildly curious.

After her reaction to his question, he was determined to find out what was going on.

It was sometime later that Noah moved slightly in his lounge chair, only half conscious of the itching tingle between his shoulder blades. He wanted suddenly to turn and look behind him, feeling just as he had after he'd heard the eerie moan in the night.

Then he heard the sound again, this time in broad daylight.

His scalp tingled a primitive warning, and muscles bunched in the instinctive reaction to a threat more sensed than seen. Slowly, carefully, Noah turned his head—and then froze.

The animal standing only a foot away was a yellowish-gray in color, and was somewhere around nine feet long. It weighed every ounce of four hundred pounds—all of it clearly muscle. Shaggy hair a shade darker than the rest framed a large, square head in which yellow eyes surveyed Noah with interest. And a long tail with a tuft of black hair on the tip waved gently.

Noah knew a moment of incredibly clear thought—sharpened by fear, he decided later—and realized that this was Caliban. And there was indeed something special Alex had neglected to mention about her pet.

She hadn't mentioned he was a lion.

Logic told him that she would hardly make a pet of

a savage creature. but logic instantly amended the thought. What would Alex. an animal trainer for four years. consider a savage creature?

Then Caliban yawned mightily. and Noah suddenly relaxed.

Where sharp teeth should have been was only the clean pink line of gums. He didn't have a single tooth in his head.

"As you can see." Alex said quietly. having obviously just reached the pool. "Cal would have a hard time turning into a maneater."

Noah tore his gaze from the lion and looked at her. "Why the hell didn't you tell me?" he demanded softly.

Caliban padded to the edge of the pool. crouched. and jumped into the water.

Alex sat in a lounge chair beside Noah's. tense with the worry that her landlord and employer might report her. She didn't think he would. but she wasn't at all sure of that. And even though a part of her cursed her own forgetfulness in neglecting to fasten the screen at her patio door. another part knew that Noah would have found out soon anyway.

"Why?" he repeated after an incredulous glance toward the swimming lion.

"Because it's illegal." she said simply. "If the animal control people knew about Caliban. he'd be put in a zoo—or destroyed."

"How long have you had him?"

"Six years."

"Since the circus?" Noah shook his head bemusedly. "But how—"

"I stole him." Alex sighed. "It's a long story."

"I've got time."

After a moment Alex nodded. "All right. But I have to go back to the beginning. Caliban's beginning. He was born in a private zoo and hand-reared because his mother died. The man who owned the zoo let Cal roam free in his house and treated him like a child." She smiled faintly, gazing toward the still-swimming lion. "As far as Cal was concerned, he was people—he didn't know he was . . . king of the beasts.

"You see, mother nature made a slight genetic error when she created Cal. She put the soul of a kitten into a lion's body. Even years later, when the zoo was closed after the owner's death and Cal was bought by a circus, he never showed an affinity for other lions. He never even learned how to roar.

"By the time I joined the circus, they'd given up on making him seem ferocious. He was too lazy to perform in the ring; they used him as a comedian, because he'd always roll over to have his belly scratched and make the crowd laugh."

"Why did you steal him?" Noah asked, watching her profile intently.

For a moment Alex didn't answer. She waited until Caliban caught the top step of the ladder and nimbly pulled himself out of the pool, then came to sprawl in a wet and lazy heap beside her lounge chair. Then she looked at Noah.

"Just before I left the circus, Cal lost all his teeth. It was partly age and partly a gum disease. He was old even then. The owner decided he'd be too much trouble to feed. so he planned to have him destroyed." Her hand dropped to rest on the broad head of her pet. "I couldn't bear that. Except for the loss of his teeth. Cal was perfectly healthy. So. the night I left the circus. I took him with me."

"The circus didn't report it?"

"No. The owner was something of a shady character: he wouldn't have dared report the loss of a big cat to the police. Besides. he knew. He knew I'd taken Cal."

She looked back down at the lion. then stared at Noah defiantly. "Lions rarely live to be twenty: Cal is thirty-one. *Thirty-one*. He has never in his life so much as scratched another living creature. and when they put him in a cage with a lioness. all he wanted to do was wash her face. as if she were a pet. He doesn't know he's a lion."

Noah realized that she was waiting for him to announce his intentions. Would he report the lion or join her in a quiet conspiracy? Instead of doing that. Noah asked another question. "How've you managed to hide him for six years?"

Alex took a deep breath and let it out slowly. "Caution. planning—and a little help from a few friends. Cal's own nature helped. Male lions tend to rest and sleep nearly twenty hours out of every twenty-four. and Cal is very obedient. He tends to stay where I put him. I take him out for exercise very early and very late. And I've been lucky."

"What d'you feed him?"

"Mostly baby food. but he'll eat anything as long as

it's finely ground. Left to themselves. lions eat only about once a week—and then they stuff themselves. But Cal's fed twice a day." She took another deep breath. then asked tightly. "What will you do?"

Noah gazed at her for a long moment. What he saw was a beautiful. delicate woman who might have weighed a fourth of what her pet weighed. a woman who had kept a lion safe. happy. and secret for six years—in a *city.* That alone spoke volumes for her strength and determination.

He rose to his feet and reached for the pale-blue terry-cloth robe lying over the back of his lounge chair. "Why don't we take Cal inside." he said mildly. "before one of the painters looks down here and has a heart attack."

Alex got up as he did. and if he had wanted to be rewarded. her glowing smile was more than he would have asked for. "You won't report it?"

"Report what?" he asked blandly. "As far as I'm concerned. your pet's just a big cat."

"Thank you. Noah."

"Don't mention it."

As they headed for the deck outside Alex's loft. Noah thought ruefully that this situation would have been a prime source of blackmail for an unscrupulous man. But Noah was neither unscrupulous enough. insensitive enough. nor stupid enough to attempt that ploy. Practically speaking. the two strongest reasons to avoid blackmail were clear: An unwilling. coerced Alex in any man's bed. he suspected. would be a dangerous. unpredictable thing indeed; and it would obviously be nothing short of insanity to blackmail a woman with her own lion—however toothless.

"What're you thinking?" Alex asked curiously as they stood in the living area of her loft.

He looked at her. "I was thinking of the possibilities of blackmail," he answered honestly, wondering how she'd react. Being Alex, of course she avoided any exclamations of horror and mistrust.

"You wouldn't," she said definitely, then added calmly, "Iced tea?"

"Thank you." Noah grinned to himself as he tossed his robe over a chair then sank down among the pillows on the couch. "What makes you so sure I wouldn't?" he asked, half-turning to watch her over the partition as she prepared the tea in the kitchen.

Alex didn't answer until she had handed him a glass and sat down at the end of the couch. She was more than a little disconcerted by the nearness of his lean, tanned body, especially since it was clothed only in dark-blue trunks. It occurred to her vaguely that her preoccupation with Caliban's safety had quite blinded her these last days to Noah's incredible attractiveness.

Wary of giving herself away, Alex unconsciously and automatically underwent a subtle transformation beneath Noah's fascinated gaze. Her own awareness of his attraction sent a danger signal to her brain and that brain, conditioned to meet danger with an appearance of calm and confidence, instantly sent its own signals to her body.

Her tense shoulders relaxed: her head rose with the poise of calm pride: the faint frown disappeared from her brow: and the turbulent green eyes subsided into serenity.

"Because you wouldn't blackmail me." she answered finally. dispassionately. "You wouldn't enjoy dominating me like that."

Noah. still fascinated. barely heard her. Since in his own mind her lion-taming past seemed incredible. he was very conscious of that part of her life: he immediately understood her transformation. and a part of him was elated to elicit that reaction from her. She was war . . . but she was *aware*.

After a moment he cleared his throat and murmured. "Should I growl or roll over or something?"

Startled. she blinked at him. Then. as realization sank in. she bit her lip unsteadily. "Um. I beg your pardon?"

"The whip and chair weren't physically present." he decided thoughtfully. "but somehow they were here."

"Don't be ridiculous." she managed to say. avoiding his eyes to pretend to watch Caliban as he dragged his bear from the bedroom.

"Alex." Noah said very gently. "I'm not a threat. Am I?"

She leaned forward to place her glass on the coffee table. mainly just to have something to do. Then she sat back and reluctantly turned to meet his steady. inquiring gaze. Softly. compelled to be honest by something in his eyes. she said. "Very few creatures are a threat—until they turn on you. But the possibility is always there."

"And you guard against possibilities."

"After four years in cages I don't have a scar anywhere," she said, steady. "Because I was always alert to the possibilities."

"I would never hurt you." He heard his own voice emerge quietly and was dimly aware that the tables had been turned on them again—by his doing this time; what could have been light was now very serious.

"You know what they say about the road to hell."

"Being paved with good intentions?" He hesitated, searching her face intently. Once more he had an odd feeling of déjà vu; their words seemed to echo in his ears as if he had heard them before and, curiously, a line from *The Tempest* whispered in his mind: *"What's past is prologue."*

"You're staring at me," she murmured, uncomfortable.

Noah shook his head slightly, not denying her accusation but rather trying to throw off the peculiar thoughts. When he gazed into her green eyes, the thoughts—any thoughts—vanished of their own will. "It just isn't fair," he said huskily, leaning forward briefly to set his glass on the coffee table.

"What?" she asked, bemused.

His hand rose to touch her cheek. "That anyone should have eyes like that."

Alex couldn't look away, not even with her instinct for self-preservation clamoring a strident warning.

And none of her other instincts would surface to protect her now because no bluff could overpower his own strength. "Noah . . ."

He leaned toward her slowly, his fingers still lightly touching her cheek. "I'm not a lion, Alex," he whispered. "I'm just a man."

As his lips found hers, she had time only to absorb the vast understatement he made with such confidence. Just a man? Then she was conscious of nothing but his touch, his kiss, and of the incredible force of the feelings rising instantly within her.

No one had ever warned her.

Vibrant colors pinwheeled before her closed eyes, so bright and shining that they made her ache. She could hear the roar of a rain-swelled stream, and smell the dark green of a forest. Then the crackle of a fire and the warm shelter of strong arms held her spellbound, enchanted. A fierce certainty gripped her body, the certainty, the familiarity, of coming home. . . .

Alex opened her eyes, dazed, to look into his equally blurred and bewildered stare. Very slowly Noah sat back, his uneven breathing obvious.

"I'll risk it," he said finally, deeply.

She swallowed. "Risk what?"

"The possibility that I'm . . . not your blue-ribbon affair."

"Noah—"

"I'll risk it, Alex. Will you?"

The blue of his eyes compelled her, pushed her past

any thoughts of safe uninvolvement. "I . . . don't think I have a choice."

"Because you're not sure? Because I could be?"

She nodded. "I thought I'd know right away." It was a tacit denial of the knowledge, and only partly a lie. She knew it was a blue-ribbon affair for her. But was it the same for him?

Noah seemed to relax. "We have time," he murmured as if to himself. He studied her for a moment, then smiled and abruptly changed the subject. "Tell me, did you learn to tell fortunes in that circus?"

Alex blinked at the change of subject, but was grateful for the opportunity to avoid serious thought. "Not really. Oh, there was an old woman with the circus who claimed to be a Gypsy—and might have been, for all I know—but that stuff's mostly fake. She talked to me a little about palmistry."

He held out his right hand, palm up, and the blue eyes laughed. "Then tell me if I'll meet someone tiny, blond, and beautiful . . ." he challenged her.

She laughed in spite of herself, but bent forward to study his hand. One neat oval nail traced the line curving at the base of his thumb, hesitating for an instant before continuing on until the line met those at the inside of his wrist. "You have a long lifeline," she murmured.

"Is there a blonde in it?" he asked gravely.

Alex sat back and smiled easily at him, her muddled emotions held strictly under control. "If there is, she didn't announce herself."

"Some fortune-teller you are," he complained.

The thud of footsteps on the stairs outside the loft caught their attention, and Alex glanced at a nearby clock. "Lunchtime; the painters are leaving. I wonder if they've finished with your loft."

"I'll take a look while I change," he said, getting up and reaching for his robe. "If so, and your loft is next, we can put Caliban in one of the other lofts until they're finished. That okay with you?"

"Fine," Alex replied casually.

"How d'you feel about hamburgers for lunch?" he asked, shrugging into the robe. "I have a grill. Some-where."

"Mine's unpacked, and I feel just fine about ham-burgers. Go change."

Noah smiled at her, a new and disturbing intensity in his eyes, then cheerfully left her loft.

After a long moment Alex slowly lifted her right hand and stared at the palm. Then she got to her feet and headed for her bedroom. "I am going round the bend," she told Caliban as she passed him, her voice definite. "The man's driven me crazy; that's the only answer." Leaving her pet alone while she went to change, Alex wished she believed her own words.

Because she didn't believe in fate.

Four

"Your brothers would kill me if they found us here."

She laughed and tossed her head, black curls falling down her back and green eyes brilliant with the half-wild spirit he loved. "They don't trust you," she confirmed merrily. "They say the son of an earl would never wed a Gypsy girl."

"They're wrong," he said huskily, pulling her down beside him on a bed of green moss. "You're mine, Tina. You'll always be mine."

She laughed again softly, exultant because he would always be hers. . . .

Alex came awake with a start, her heart pounding erratically. Sleeping in the middle of the day? But she never napped and—Lord!—what dreams!

"You were smiling in your sleep," Noah said softly. "What were you dreaming about?"

She sat up on the lounge and self-consciously tugged the slipping neckline of her peasant blouse up over a bare shoulder. "Oh, nothing important," she said evasively.

They had grilled hamburgers outside and then hidden Cal in one of the empty lofts before the painters returned from their own lunch. The paint smell still remained in Noah's loft, and since the painters were now in Alex's loft, they could hardly remain there. Shaded by a makeshift awning beside the pool, they'd elected to stay outside.

Noah, raised on an elbow in his own lounge chair, was smiling at her. "You look very young when you sleep. Very innocent."

Alex wanted to avoid the warmth in his vivid blue eyes, but found herself unable to look away. Disturbed by the thought of him watching her sleep, she changed the subject. "You never told me what kind of photographic work you do."

"Didn't I?" He was still smiling, but allowed the change of subject. "Basically I photograph whatever I'm asked to. Hotels and resorts for their postcards and brochures. Buildings for advertisements. People, of course: family groups, publicity stills and the like. Even animals."

"I'll have to see how you do with Cal as a subject."

"He's probably a ham."

Alex laughed. "As a matter of fact, he is."

"I'd like to photograph you," Noah said.

A shout from her loft saved Alex the necessity of responding, and she was soon busy inside the building. The painters were working quickly to get the first two lofts finished, and a crew of carpenters had started the finish work on two of the other lofts. The foreman of the crew had to consult both Alex and Noah on the placement of walls and doorways since Noah had discovered that his architect had taken liberties with the plans, rendering them almost useless.

Decisions made, the crew got down to work. Alex was kept busy between the painters and carpenters, especially since Noah had approved several inexpensive additions she had suggested to individualize each loft. She spent an hour dashing up and down the stairs with the sketches she'd drawn up for the workers' benefit, busy out of habit, interest in the subject, and a desire to avoid thinking about anything else.

As usual, she did more than her own work. Union representatives would most likely have been appalled, but not a single member of either crew objected.

In the middle of everything Noah went upstairs, unpacked and loaded one of his cameras, and then came back down to literally blend in with the woodwork until no one noticed him. It was innate, that ability, but also one he had worked to perfect; both people and animals, he'd found, responded much better to a camera they weren't aware of.

So Noah made himself virtually invisible, the soft sounds his camera made undetectable in the general melée. And at several points during the afternoon he wished he had a tape recorder as well, because the process whereby Alex turned herself into both a painter and a carpenter boasted sound effects and dialogue every bit as amusing and fascinating as the images he was steadily capturing on film.

"Who told Alex she could use pliers to get nails out of the walls?"

"She didn't ask, boss, or I would've—"

"Never mind. Here, Alex, take this hammer. No! Don't— It's all right, Alex, I'm sure you didn't break Willie's toe. No, he's always that color. Aren't you, Willie?"

"You said *green* for this room, Alex. What? That *is* green! Well, maybe not *green* green, but— All right, all right. Just get off the ladder, please."

"Here, Alex, wear these coveralls. Because I'm paying my men to *work*, not look at your legs, that's why."

"Boss, we'd never—"

"Shut up, Willie. You were looking harder than anybody. See, Alex, I told you he was always that color."

"Sam? Sam? Alex, what'd you do with Sam? Well, what's he doing in the closet? Hiding from you? Nonsense. Sam, come out of there. Where'd you get the shiner? Oh. Well, it isn't Alex's fault you ran into her elbow; you shouldn't have been in her way."

"Alex! Where'd you learn words like that? Wipe that grin off your face, Willie!"

"The wallpaper isn't upside down, Alex, I promise. I'm sure. I'm *positive*. Do the flowers in my garden do what? Oh. No, I guess they don't grow upside down at that. Fix the wallpaper, Sam."

"Get off the ladder, Alex. Because my insurance doesn't cover you, that's why. Look, I don't care if you did trapeze work in a circus— What? You did? Well . . . there's no net. Get down from there."

By the end of the afternoon Noah had used several rolls of film. He had also come to a better understanding of the bewildered expressions two of Alex's former clients had worn. Throughout the day he had watched her win the exasperated affection of a dozen working men, had heard her tiny voice swearing with the cheerful fluency of a sailor, and had seen her throw herself into the work with enthusiasm—never mind that she didn't know what she was doing half the time.

Any of these workmen, Noah thought in amusement, would have been happy to go out and slay dragons for her. But after a day in her company, each would have made certain she was locked in the castle before they sallied forth to do battle for her.

Otherwise there would have been a few roasted knights.

Alex had always had the capacity to focus all her attention on whatever she was doing at the moment, particularly if it was something she was interested in, or something new to her experience. Because of that, she was aware of Noah's activities with his camera only at the end of the day when—she strongly suspected—he decided to let her know what he was doing.

The painters and carpenters were packing up for the day, and Alex returned the coveralls loaned to her before turning to find Noah leaning against a wall with his camera hanging around his neck.

"You didn't say I couldn't," he reminded her, grinning.

"How long have you been taking pictures?" she asked uneasily.

"All afternoon. Got some dandy shots too."

They were in her loft, which was cluttered again since all the furniture had been pushed into the middle of the large room and covered with huge sheets of canvas. Alex wandered over to her couch and lifted a corner of the canvas. She picked up one of the colorful pillows and held it in both hands as she gazed at Noah consideringly.

"That," she told him, "was not nice."

Noah found himself instinctively looking around for something to hide behind, and had to grin again. "Are you going to throw the pillow at me?" he asked politely.

With a sigh Alex dropped the pillow and sank down on the couch. "When I decide to start throwing pillows, you won't have any warning. You won't even have time to duck."

"I can hardly wait."

Alex gave him a rueful look, then frowned as her eyes turned to the couch.

"What is it?" Noah asked, coming forward.

She was watching the canvas covering the couch. Or, more correctly, she was watching something underneath the canvas. "We've got company," she observed thoughtfully.

Noah watched a small lump move erratically beneath the canvas beside Alex. Before he could suggest she move in case it was a snake or something, she swept back the canvas to reveal their "company." It was a tiny white kitten with a smudge of black on his nose and brilliant green eyes. With a squeak the kitten lurched the remaining few inches to Alex, climbed fiercely into her lap, and began to purr with astonishing volume.

"Where'd he come from?" Noah asked.

"Beats me." Alex got up, holding the kitten securely in one hand, and went into the kitchen to find food.

"The doors have been open all day; I suppose he just wandered in." She watched the thin little creature hungrily lapping milk after nearly falling headfirst into the bowl, then lifted her gaze to Noah. "If I can't find out whom he belongs to, I'll have to keep him."

"I had a feeling," Noah murmured. "You aren't the type to cart him off to the animal shelter. How will Cal react?"

"Oh, he loves babies," Alex answered, looking back down at the kitten. "He'll probably try to wash the fur right off this one."

Noah turned and headed purposefully for the door.

"Was it something I said?" Alex asked, half-laughing.

"I'm out of film," Noah said over his shoulder. "And I have to have photos of this meeting!"

Noah got some wonderful shots of the tiny white kitten, back arched and tail bristling, meeting a distant cousin many times his size. Photos of the cautious, gentle advances of Cal. And finally, within an hour or so, he got photos of a tiny, purring bundle of white fur curled trustingly between the tremendous paws of an adoring lion.

Noah spent half the night setting up his darkroom.

"I love this one."

Alex reached for the picture that had collected four wolf whistles as it was passed from hand to hand among the carpenters. She had been gone all morning running errands in town, arriving back home only seconds before to find all the men gathered in the hallway grinning over a stack of eight-by-ten photographs. For a fearful instant Alex thought that Noah might have forgotten himself and handed over the pictures of Cal and the kitten. But she immediately saw that all these photos were of people.

Mostly her. The picture that all the men were admiring was of her. She was halfway up a ladder, bent forward over the top and waving a sheaf of papers in the patient face of the foreman. He had his hands on his hips, his face nearly level with hers in spite of her added height, and Noah had snapped the photo at the exact instant the foreman had cast a wary glance at the hammer Alex held in her free hand.

What the men had whistled at, she realized, was the part of the picture showing long golden legs exposed by a pair of just barely decent shorts. She leafed through the remaining pictures, finding herself the focus of each one. And she realized that either Noah was a very good photographer or else had been awfully lucky, because every shot was a beauty. The one she stared at the longest was of herself. Noah had captured something she'd never even seen in a mirror.

In the photo she was leaning back against a doorjamb and glancing up as a shaft of bright sunlight fell on her from one of the high windows. Alex couldn't remember the moment, but she realized that she must have been deep in thought, her mind caught up with plans. Her eyes were wide, her face dreamy and wearing a wistful half smile. She looked more beautiful than she knew herself to be, curiously softened and elusive. But there was something in her eyes, a glint of something that was more than mischief or spirit.

Or maybe that was just a trick of light.

Alex gazed at the picture for long moments, feeling a peculiar sense of seeing someone else instead of herself. Then she shook the feeling away and looked up to discover that she was alone in the hallway; the crews had returned to work.

Leaving her various parcels where she'd dropped them, Alex headed up the stairs. She checked in on Cal and the as-yet-unnamed kitten, making certain they were still safe and safely locked in one of the lofts. They were fine, both sound asleep and the kitten curled up in Cal's mane as he sprawled on his side. She went on up and finally tracked Noah down in his darkroom; his front door was open and paperhangers were busy in the bathroom. The door to the darkroom was closed, a sign hand-lettered on a piece of cardboard and thumbtacked to the door announcing merely: KEEP OUT!

Alex knocked. "It's me, Noah."

"Out in a second." he called.

She leaned against the wall, still holding the photos and glancing around the loft. Noah's loft was double the size of the others, running the entire length of the building. It was divided in half, the hallway door opening into the living area. Where the rest of the building had solid brick walls dividing two lofts on each floor, Noah's was divided by a plasterboard wall and an arched entrance into his work area.

Alex was in the work area; the darkroom had been converted from what would have been a bedroom. The second bathroom on this floor had remained, Noah said, because he sometimes used models in his work and a room for them to change or apply makeup was necessary. The raised platform along the street side was cluttered with large filing cabinets, various bits of furniture and other props, but the remainder of the large room was mostly bare. There was no kitchen on this side, which added to the floor space.

Alex was gazing around and thinking vaguely of white walls to increase available light and large screens of various colors that Noah could use as backgrounds if he chose. The painters had already finished with the living area of this loft, but had yet to reach the work area.

She jumped in surprise when arms surrounded her from behind and a kiss landed just beneath her right ear.

"Hello," Noah said gaily. "Errands finished?"

Alex silently ordered her heart to quit pounding. It didn't work. "Um . . . yes. I've got more swatches and wallpaper samples for you to look at."

"Later," Noah suggested.

She turned to face him, managing to step back and wave the photos in his face to distract him. "You wasted film."

"I don't consider it a waste." He looked suddenly hurt. "You don't like the pictures?"

"I didn't say that. I said you wasted film. Do all photographers take so many shots of one subject?"

Noah crossed his arms over his chest and leaned back against the wall. "They do," he said, "if one subject wears many faces."

She frowned at him.

"That's one face," he noted consideringly, a gleam of laughter in his almost-silver eyes. Then he laughed aloud. "Sprite, you wear more faces than a gallery of paintings."

Alex managed to hold on to the frown. "Sprite?"

He nodded. "An elf or pixie. 'Course, it also means a ghost, and you do have a—haunting way about you."

She chose to take him literally. "I don't rattle chains in the night."

"No, but you haunt my dreams."

Alex cleared her throat strongly and looked down at the pictures she still held. "This one's very good," she murmured.

"It's my favorite," he agreed. "Five parts wistful innocence, three parts elusiveness, and two parts evil."

"Evil?" Alex stared down at the picture of herself, then looked at him. "I don't see any evil."

"You wouldn't." Before she could respond, he was going on judiciously. "Just a touch, mind you, a certain look in the eyes. It's no easier to define than Mona Lisa's smile, but any man would call it evil. If I could photograph a siren, she'd have that look."

Alex had the feeling it was a compliment, but wasn't at all sure. And she didn't want to ask. "Oh."

"I like it," he told her in a consoling tone.

She was trying hard to define the look in *his* eyes. It was, she thought dimly, rather like the way a hurricane would look trapped in a silver-blue bottle; a tremendous force of nature caged. It made her nervous.

Noah smiled slowly. "You've picked up your whip and chair again," he said.

"You were roaring." Alex knew it was a ridiculous comment to make, but Noah was laughing.

"Was I? Funny, I didn't hear anything."

She swallowed a laugh of her own. "You saw my whip and chair; I heard your roar."

"What is this, *Wild Kingdom*?" asked a bewildered voice from the archway leading to the living area.

Alex and Noah turned hastily, both momentarily uncomfortable because their imagery was definitely private and not for outsiders. They found themselves confronting a petite young woman walking toward them. She was dressed as casually as they in jeans and a light sweater with the sleeves pushed up to her elbows. Her bright hair was so red it looked unreal, and overlarge horn-rimmed glasses framed big, spaniellike brown eyes.

No one would ever call her beautiful, but there was an endearing freshness about her cute face. She was the "girl next door."

And Alex had the oddest impulse to say, But you should be taller! Bewildered by the urge, she pushed it out of her mind.

"The guys downstairs told me I could find the owner up here," she told them briskly, the earlier question clearly a rhetorical one.

"I'm the owner," Noah said, and accepted a business card from her automatically. He looked at the card. His lips twitched once, but his glance at Alex was grave as he handed her the card. He introduced himself and Alex as she read the card.

Alex instantly understood his brief amusement; the name on the card read: Theodora Suzanne Jessica Tyler. *Good Lord,* Alex thought, *another little woman cursed with a big name!* But then she read the remainder of the card, and her amusement was chased away by a chill.

Department of Animal Control.

"What can I do for you, Miss Tyler?" Noah asked politely.

"I'm checking on a report of some kind of large animal. Have either of you seen anything?"

"I saw a German shepherd this morning," Noah offered. "He was big."

Theodora Suzanne Jessica Tyler gave him a look. "Not a pet, Mr. Thorne. According to the report, this animal may have escaped from a circus or zoo. The lady who called in was definitely rattled, but she thought what she saw may have been a lion."

Alex wished their visitor had overheard *anything* except the wonderfully suggestive lion-tamer imagery. She kept her face politely blank with an effort, her heart pounding.

Noah was frowning. "A lion? Loose in San Francisco?"

"Could be. No report of one escaping, but sometimes people are funny about reporting things like that."

"We'll certainly keep an eye out, then."

"Thank you." The response was automatic and polite, but the shrewd brown eyes were glancing between them thoughtfully. Then she changed the subject, and her voice was friendly. "So you're converting this building to lofts?"

"In the process," Noah said easily.

"I'm looking for a place. When will you be ready for tenants?"

"A few weeks, I think."

"Good. I'll check back with you. As a matter of fact, I'll probably be hanging around for a while. The neighborhood, I mean. There aren't too many places a lion could be hidden, but there are a few. Large, mostly empty buildings. Like this one, for instance."

Noah's laugh sounded perfectly natural. "I think I'd know if there was a lion hiding out in this building, Miss Tyler."

She smiled brilliantly. "Yes, I suppose you would at that. Well, it was nice meeting you. If you see anything, give me a call."

"Sure."

They stood perfectly still for long moments, then Noah headed for the hallway to make certain their visitor had left. When he came back, he found Alex sitting on the edge of the raised platform, her face a little pale.

"That," she said softly, "is the closest brush I've ever had."

He sat down beside her. "I hate to say it, but I don't think that's the last we'll see of her, Alex."

She glanced at the card still in her hand, then showed him a crooked smile. "Ladies with impressive names tend to try to live up to them. I can vouch for that. She'll be back."

Noah was worried about Caliban's possible exposure, but he was more worried that Alex would fade into the misty night in order to save her pet. He looked at her steadily. "D'you plan on . . . living to fight another day?"

She laid aside the photos and business card, then slid off the platform and began pacing restlessly. "You mean am I going to run?"

"It crossed my mind that you might leave," he said evenly. "After all, Cal's been a part of your life for years. I can barely claim a few weeks."

Alex stood in the archway, listening as the sounds of shouts and laughter echoed up the stairs; the workmen were heading for lunch. "If they find out about Cal, you'll be in trouble too," she reminded him.

"I'm not afraid of trouble." Noah joined her in the archway.

She moved slightly, a restless, troubled gesture. "I don't want to turn you into a liar, Noah."

He chuckled softly. "It's reversed."

"What?" She looked at him.

" 'Would she could make of me a saint or I of her a sinner,' " he quoted. "It's reversed for us. But I don't mind, Alex. If you were endangering anyone, I'd mind. But you aren't. And I'm more than willing to help you hide your lion and keep him safe."

". . . *soldier in the barn . . . must keep him safe . . .*"

Alex blinked, seeing, for a jarring instant, a dusty blue uniform and blue eyes shot with gray that gazed on her with quiet thanks. Then the image vanished and it was Noah looking down at her, his gray-blue eyes steady.

She opened her mouth to ask him something. But the question never even formed in her mind. He'd think she was crazy, she decided. And maybe she was. Or maybe . . . maybe she had hidden Noah once, a very long time ago, and now he was returning the favor by helping her to hide Caliban.

Or maybe she needed her head examined. By an expert.

"Alex?" He was holding her shoulders gently.

"If you think we can pull it off," she said huskily, "I'm willing to give it a try. It's not easy to hide a four-hundred-pound lion though."

"We'll manage. I promise you we will." He smiled down at her. "Now, why don't you go check on your cats while I start lunch?"

It stormed again that night, and the building lost

"I was r
His sig
hoping tc
"I'd nev
"Then I
"Wome
"Set a
trailblaze
Alex loc
shadowe
felt a sud
or the te
bering th
have beei
the imag
tion end
Had he ri
his way
apart?
Had he
Draggi
focused
shoulder
he gazec
tainty.
"Lousy
"Mayb
"No, I
"Hit?"
"Vietn
tone.

power once more. Prepared this time, Alex and Noah retreated to his loft and built a fire in the fireplace the mason had unblocked the week before. The two cats remained in Alex's loft with a battery-powered lantern for company.

The firelight cast strange shadows in the huge room, and since the storm had brought suddenly cold wind with it, they were both glad to sit close to the hearth with pillows borrowed from Alex's couch and a thick quilt to guard against the chilly floor.

"Carpet," Noah said firmly.

"But the floor's beautiful wood and you had it refinished," Alex objected.

"It's cold. Carpet."

"You were going to carpet only the platform."

"I changed my mind. I'm going to carpet from wall to wall."

"Well, I want wood floors in my loft."

Noah sipped his wine and grinned at her. "Then I hope you plan to have a rug by your bed, or you'll get a nasty jolt every morning. Or do you sleep in socks?"

"No, I don't sleep in socks. But this place has central heating."

"Central heating that goes out during a storm— and I'll bet we're going to have plenty of storms."

"Pessimist."

"Realist. Now that I've become a landlord, I expect *everything* to go wrong."

Alex giggled, then looked suspiciously at the level of wine in the nearly empty bottle nearby. "Are you trying to get me drunk?" she asked Noah bluntly.

"I ar
to the
have b
She
finish
drunk
"Yes
She
him, "
"A d
"Wh
"I ju
"Oh
might
man.'
"Sta
"Sto
"It w
Alex
tage o
kill yo
He e
that y
clear,
troubl
"I ca
"No.
Alex
"I se
could
plead

Five

He could see between the slats, watch as the rebel soldiers questioned the slender woman standing before their horses. It was hot and dusty within the barn, and especially here in this corncrib. He could feel the bristly weight of the corncobs, smell the dry, musty scent of them.

Thank God they didn't need feed for their mounts.

His shoulder ached and he wanted to shift position. He knew he was bleeding again, and that he was feverish. The woman would change the filthy bandage when the soldiers were gone.

If she didn't turn him in.

He was desperately tired. And hungry. But, more than anything else, he was sick of war. He longed for the beauty of rolling green pastures and the sweet smell of cut hay drying in the summer sun. He kept

74

his squinting eyes on the woman, unable to look past her at fields devastated by war, or at the house behind her, the house that had once looked graceful and dignified but now bore scars of war in its broken windows and pitted bricks.

Why was she helping him? Because he reminded her of a brother the war had taken from this place? Or a husband? How many of her men, he wondered, had she lost in a cause that was hopeless?

The sound of hooves recalled his feverish wits, and he heard his own ragged sigh as he watched the mounted men riding away. The woman stood where she was until even their dust was gone, then hurried into the house. He waited, too weary to push himself out from under the pile of corn. He waited and, after a time, he saw her come out of the house and hurry toward the barn, a bundle in her arms.

And the sun shone down on her blond hair, reminding him of golden wheat in a rolling field. . . .

Noah woke abruptly, feeling disoriented. Dreaming, he thought. But whose dreams? Rebel soldiers and a blond woman? He shook his head, puzzled, only then becoming aware of the warm woman whose head rested on his shoulder. He looked down at blond curls and then rested his chin in the softness, vaguely aware that the power was back on and a couple of lamps lighted the room. He could barely hear the hum of the central heating, and wondered when the fire had gone out.

Not that it mattered. They were warm. He tightened his arm around the slender body at his side, marveling that he was able to sleep while holding her. He wanted her. Dear heaven, how he wanted her! Just the sight of her made his body ache, and his mind . . . His mind! He couldn't think straight in her presence, and it always surprised him that he could string words together to make a coherent sentence.

He felt like a teenager tripping over his feet and over his tongue, uncertain of himself and awestruck by her. His blood pressure skyrocketed and his pulse hammered like a machine-gun when she smiled at him, and every instinct he could claim shrieked at him to grab her and hold on forever.

Noah had never felt so strongly before. His own emotions washed over him like an ocean's relentless waves, nearly drowning him.

How much longer could he pull on a cheerful smile or dredge up teasing words when he wanted so desperately to groan out his love and his need and carry her away somewhere?

For as long as it took.

A blue-ribbon affair? She was that to him. And so much more. She was the pot of gold at the end of the rainbow. Spring after a harsh winter. The lovely, rain-washed quiet after a storm.

He wanted to tell her that, but caution held him silent. She was a woman who believed life was built on change; how long could he hold her? How could he dare to hope this lovely, wandering sprite would choose to remain at his side?

Noah swallowed hard and felt the harsh rasp of his dry throat. Determination welled up inside of him, easing the ache born of fear. He'd find a way. Somehow, he would convince her to stay.

If it took forever.

He held her close and shut his eyes, holding her for now.

When Alex woke to find herself clinging like a limpet to Noah's sleeping body, she didn't know whether to laugh or cry. It was encouraging to realize that he was holding her rather tightly, but the possibility of him awakening to find her so close made her feel oddly shy.

She had never in her life slept in a man's arms.

Carefully, gently, Alex moved away and slipped from beneath the quilt, pausing only when he murmured something and followed the words with a curiously broken sound. She knelt gazing at his face for a few moments, absorbed by the shadow of his morning beard, the long lashes that were dark crescents against his tanned skin.

After a while she rose and silently left his loft, going down the stairs to her own. It was nearly dawn, a chill, silent dawn, and she felt as if she were the only living soul awake and aware. It was a very lonely feeling, and it surprised her because she had always gotten up early and alone.

In her own loft she found a Windbreaker and took Cal out for his run, leaving his small friend lapping milk in the kitchen. She was more cautious than usual, eyes and ears straining to catch any indication of trouble. Whoever had reported seeing a lion, she thought, must have been up late at night or early in the morning; she would have to be doubly watchful from now on. She took special care to hide or erase all signs of her pet's morning romp.

She looked up just as they turned back to the building, and saw Noah silhouetted by the lamps behind him as he stood at his balcony doors. It was dawn, and she was sure he could see them. She lifted a hand and watched him acknowledge the gesture with a wave, then she headed for her loft.

Back inside, she fed Cal and then took a long, hot shower, trying to shake off the last of the night's peculiar feelings. But they wouldn't go away. She stood before the vanity in her bathroom and stared at the fogged image of herself, restless.

Restlessness had always meant it was time to change. To move on, to try a different job or cut her hair or move the furniture. Now, for the first time, Alex wondered if she had gotten her own motivation wrong all these years. Was it change her restlessness had urged, or had she been searching for something she hadn't been able to name?

For ten years she'd been either literally or figuratively on the move. Ever since a visit to a circus had tugged at the mind and heart of a sixteen-year-old, she had moved from place to place, from one job to another. Contentment for a while, then restlessness and change.

Today she was restless, but she didn't want to move on. This, she thought, was a different kind of uneasiness. Not discontent, but rather the tense hesitation of someone about to make an important decision. A part of her insisted the decision was made, but Alex was afraid to put it into words. She was afraid because she had never in her life reached out to anyone else. She'd been a temperamental orphan who had refused to allow herself to be comforted after a scraped knee or bruised heart; she'd grown into a woman who was wary of reaching for someone who might not be there.

She wasn't accustomed to casual touches, to hugs or kisses or arms holding her in the night.

Alex watched the mirror fog up even more, and realized her own tears were blurring her vision. Swearing softly, she dashed the moisture away and went to start breakfast.

When she answered Noah's knock a few minutes later, Alex was under control and calm. "Hi," she said. "Ready for breakfast?"

"Are you offering?" he asked with a ridiculously hopeful expression.

"It's the least I can do for my boss." She closed the door behind him, her control faltering for a moment as she wondered a bit wildly why the man had to be so damned *handsome*!

"You abandoned your boss at the crack of dawn," he chided her.

"Sorry. Had to walk the cat."

Noah paused near the couch to look at the picture

of a small white kitten atop Cal's broad head and chewing busily on his ear. "Damn. Wish I had my camera."

"Coffee?"

"Thanks." He accepted the cup she held out, sipping the hot liquid and watching her move gracefully on the other side of the low partition. "I didn't take advantage, sprite," he said suddenly, his tone light.

"You were a perfect gentleman," she agreed, matching his tone in spite of the tightness in her throat.

Very softly he said, "Then why the whip and chair?"

Alex busied herself turning strips of sizzling bacon. It gave her a moment to think, but she still couldn't answer that question. Instead, she sent him a wry glance and said, "Seven in the morning and the man's asking cryptic questions."

"Was that cryptic? Sorry. Maybe I should have asked why you're a few hundred miles away from me this morning."

"Not that far, surely." Alex was suddenly aware of his presence directly behind her, but she was nonetheless startled when he slid his arms around her waist and pulled her back against him.

"Hey, she's real," Noah said quietly. "She's not a figment of your imagination, old sport. Or a ghost. Just a very elusive lady with an invisible whip and chair."

"Noah, you're making me burn the bacon," she managed to say.

"Wouldn't want to do that, would we?" He released her and stepped back.

Alex turned suddenly and caught his hand before he could move away. "Noah . . ." She looked at him, at his still face and curiously guarded eyes, and she dredged up a self-mocking smile from somewhere. On a half-laughing sigh, she murmured, "Stop *roaring!*"

His fingers tightened around hers and his still face relaxed in a faint smile. "King of the beasts. Unlike Cal, I have all my teeth. And nobody put a kitten in me. Show me a lioness, and I'm afraid I'd want to do more than just wash her face. But I'd never hurt her, Alex. I'd never hurt her." His blue-gray eyes were very direct and very steady.

She remembered the soldier in blue and someone else, someone holding a Gypsy girl on a bed of green moss. She didn't know what it meant, or if it meant anything at all. But she knew what she felt. And caution was only a dull ache pushed aside.

"Why don't you set the table?" she suggested, the restlessness gone. Decision made and confronted. Instinct, she knew, might well conjure up her whip and chair, but she would never again knowingly hold Noah at a distance.

He lifted her hand briefly to his lips, still wearing that half smile. But his eyes were brighter, as if he knew or sensed a difference between them. He went to set the table.

Alex watched him for a moment, then turned back to her burned bacon. And her burned bridges.

*   *   *

By the time breakfast was finished, the workmen had arrived with the usual clatter. Alex barely had time to nip up the stairs and hide Cal and the kitten she'd begun calling Buddy, for want of a better name, in one of the empty lofts and lock the door securely.

Within an hour the building was ringing with the sounds of shouts and hammers and the clashing of ladders and paint cans. Traffic jams began occurring on the stairs as masons arrived to finish repairing the remaining fireplaces, and men came to measure for carpet, and landscapers kept popping inside to ask Noah where he wanted a particular bush or tree.

Alex had to sneak Cal and the kitten out of one loft and into another at one point because the masons were about to move into the one they had been inhabiting. She managed the feat, but couldn't control a startled jump when she ran into Theodora Suzanne Jessica Tyler at the bottom of the stairs.

"Oh, hi," Alex managed lightly. "Noah's around somewhere."

"I don't want to bother him." The redhead smiled brightly. "I just wondered if he'd mind me wandering around inside the fence out back."

Alex shrugged casually. "You'll have to ask him, Miss Tyler. I'm just the hired help."

Shrewd brown eyes studied her, but the friendly smile remained. "Call me Teddy; the rest is too much of a mouthful."

"Sure. I'm Alex." The last thing she wanted to do

was spend too much time with someone who could take Cal away from her, but Alex was reasonably certain this lady was no quitter; she wouldn't give up easily. And if you couldn't get rid of an enemy, you turned her into a friend.

It might even work.

Cheerfully Alex confided her own impossible name, and the two were laughing over the trials and tribulations they had endured, when another voice echoed down the stairs.

"Sprite! Where *is* that woman?"

Watching Noah come down the stairs toward them, Teddy murmured, "Just the hired help?" to Alex. Before she could respond, Noah had reached them.

"Hello, Miss—Tyler, isn't it?"

"That's it. Call me Teddy. I just wanted to ask if you'd mind me wandering around out back, Mr. Thorne."

He looked blank. "It's Noah. And, no, but why? Nothing out there except trees and weeds. The landscapers haven't gotten that far yet."

"I'm still looking for my lion," Teddy said brightly. "An animal that big usually leaves some signs. I have to check out everything, you understand—rules."

"Of course."

"Thanks for the cooperation. I'll let you know if I find anything."

"Do that."

"See you, Alex."

Alex nodded, her smile firmly in place, and watched

the redhead leave the building briskly and head around back.

"Will she find anything?" Noah asked.

"If she knows what to look for." Alex drew a deep breath. "Cal's been sharpening his claws on the trees."

"I couldn't say no without arousing suspicion, Alex."

"I know." She smiled up at him. "You're the brains of the gang, pal; think of some way we can explain those scarred trees."

"I'll try, Bonnie, but these G-ladies are tough customers."

Alex couldn't help but laugh. She shook her head and changed the subject. "Did you want me for something?"

Noah caught her in his arms so that she had to clutch at his shirt to keep her balance. In a throbbing voice he said, "I dare not offer what I desire to give, much less take what I shall die to want!"

She blinked at him. "Good heavens. What's that from?"

"A paraphrase from *The Tempest.* I've become fond of that play."

Staring up at his reflective expression, Alex fought a desire to giggle. "Oh. Well, I meant, did you want me for anything special."

He looked at her, his eyes suddenly darkening to a stormy gray. "Always. Always something special."

Alex reacted without thought, her arms sliding up around his neck as his lips met hers. She tuned out the sounds of the workmen, listening only to her own heart pounding and to the hot blood rushing through her veins.

A sudden fierceness rose in her when his mouth slanted across hers hungrily; she wanted to hold him with every muscle she possessed, tie him to her, cage them together. And there was elation, an odd, giddy relief, as if she had found a treasure long lost to her.

She could feel the need building in him, and an answering need rippled through her body like the shock waves of an earthquake. His lips were branding themselves on more than her own, searing through to the deepest levels of herself until they touched and marked her soul. Alex wanted to cry out wildly, emotions spiraling inside her until they filled her, consumed her. . . .

"Excuse me, but— Oh. Sorry."

Alex stared up into clouded eyes that cleared slowly, and felt a wrenching sense of loss when Noah released her and turned to face an apologetic Teddy.

Noah cleared his throat. "Yes, Miss—Teddy?"

"The gate's locked. I looked, but there isn't another. I'm really sorry to disturb you."

"No problem." Noah glanced at Alex, his eyes still stormy. "I'll unlock it for you."

Alex remained there at the base of the stairs for a long moment, one hand gripping the railing. The sheer raw power of her response frightened her, but there was an odd satisfaction as well because she'd not known she could feel so deeply. And there was more. The rush of emotion was still with her even though he was not.

Her hand released the railing and rose, and she gazed down at her palm with a growing sense of wonder. Was it like that, then? A pairing older than either of them could know? A destiny that held no certainty except the certainty of love?

Love . . .

She caught her breath, releasing it in a ragged sigh. What could she say to Noah? *I've always loved you, even when you were a union soldier, and when I was a Gypsy girl and . . . and other places and times and people that were us.*

Lord, she couldn't tell him that! He'd think she had flipped, gone stark raving bananas! And maybe she had.

"Alex! Oh, there you are. Didn't Noah tell you? We need you up here." The painter was bending over the railing a floor above and staring down at her.

"Coming." She turned and automatically climbed the stairs, her heart thudding heavily from something other than the exercise.

Noah escorted Teddy through the gate and into the fenced area, determined to do his part to keep Cal safe. He wondered briefly at Alex's clear decision to be friendly to this woman, finally coming to the same conclusion that Alex had come to: A friendly enemy might possibly jump your way when the chips were down.

"I'll come along if you don't mind," he told her casually.

"I don't mind. It's your property, after all."

Noah followed her toward the trees and swore silently; even from here he could see the deep scars on a large oak tree. His mind clicked into gear and began working frantically. Any reason. Any reason at all. He didn't have to prove anything. She was the one who had to prove something.

Teddy halted before the tree, her eyes measuring the distance from the ground to the top of the gouges—several feet above her head.

He didn't make the mistake of jumping in with an explanation of the scars, but merely stood and looked around casually. "What do you look for when you're tracking a lion?" he asked her casually.

She pushed her hands into the back pockets of her jeans, relaxed and at ease, gazing at him steadily. "Oh, what you'd expect. Tracks. Maybe deep gouges in a tree."

Noah frowned at her for a moment, then looked at the tree. He chuckled quietly. "Sorry to disappoint you, but those weren't made by a lion."

"Oh? What, then?"

"I caught some kids out here with a hatchet one day," he answered, perjuring his soul without hesitation and ruthlessly sacrificing the reputations of the mythical kids. "They'd already gotten several of the trees, I'm afraid. God knows why."

"It does seem a senseless thing to do."

"Doesn't it? But things like that make the papers every day."

Teddy merely nodded, the shrewd brown eyes unreadable, then began walking again. Noah followed, giving silent thanks that the lot was so overgrown with weeds, there were no bare patches where a track could present unexplainable and wholly damning evidence against Cal.

Other than three more scarred trees, the lot was innocent.

Noah walked her back to and through the gate, locking it behind them and saying cheerfully, "The damge was done, but there'll be no more kids with hatchets in there."

She shook hands with him briskly. "Well, thanks for taking the trouble, Noah. I'll be seeing you." And she walked toward a small truck parked in front of the building.

Noah went inside, more troubled than relieved. He met Alex coming down the stairs and answered her quizzical look. "I told her it was kids with hatchets. She didn't believe me, but didn't question."

Alex went through the open door into her loft, and he followed. The painters having finished in there, the furniture was back in place and the canvas covers gone. She sat down on the couch, absently picking up one of the decorative pillows and hugging it. The interlude on the stairs was hardly forgotten, but she was worried about losing Cal and still unsettled by her growing belief in destiny.

"Did she say she'd be back?"

"She said she'd be seeing me. And I'm willing to bet we'll be seeing her." He sat down beside her on the couch.

"It isn't fair," she murmured. "Cal's happy with me, and he would never hurt anyone."

"Have you tried getting a special permit to keep him?"

"I never dared," she confessed. "If they turned me down, the animal control people would know about him. Besides, I've never had a place they'd consider large enough to hold a lion."

"Plenty of room here," Noah pointed out carefully. "And you certainly have the owner's permission to house a lion." He could read the worry in her taut features, and he was still afraid she'd decide to leave in order to save her lion. She smiled at him with an obvious effort, and his heart ached because she was so lovely and so vitally important to him.

"Thanks, Noah. If this whole thing goes public, it's nice to know I can count on your support."

"That you have," he confirmed lightly. "Always."

Something about his voice caused Alex to quickly change the subject. "You know, you've never told me anything about your background."

"Nothing much to tell."

"Fair trade," Alex chided him. "If I remember correctly, I told you practically everything about me when we were still strangers in the dark."

He chuckled. "Okay. What d'you want to know?"

"Everything, of course."

"Should I start with my birth, or would you settle for a more recent history?"

"Noah!"

"Sorry. Well, I was born and raised in San Francisco, the genuinely brilliant son of proud parents who now live in Seattle. I have a younger sister in college in the East, and a younger brother who's an attorney in Texas. After high school I joined the army, and after that I came back here to go to college. Since college I've traveled a bit for my work, but tend to stick pretty close to home, given a choice.

"I sleep with the window open, can't carry a tune in a bucket, and dance passably well. I was taught to pick up after myself, don't mind washing dishes or taking out the garbage, and I can cook as long as it's simple."

"And you're still running around loose?" she asked, trying not to laugh.

"I was saving myself for you," he told her in a pained voice.

"Pardon me if I doubt that. You may not have been struck by cupid's lightning, but I'll bet you wandered out into the storm a few times."

"I got my feet wet," he admitted, laughter gleaming in his eyes. "A little experience never hurts."

"Certainly not," she agreed, straight-faced. "I hate heavy-handed amateurs."

"Known a few of those, have you?"

"A few."

"Well, I don't claim to be an expert," he said, "but I'll forever deny being heavy-handed."

While he was talking calmly, Noah had taken the pillow away from her and pulled her into his lap. Alex made no attempt to resist, nor did she comment on the actions immediately. When she did comment, it was in a very dry voice.

"You may not be heavy-handed, but you're certainly a take-charge kind of man, aren't you?"

Noah smiled down at her, eyes flaring. "Patience has its limits."

"Stop roaring."

"You're imagining things."

"I am not." Alex put a hand against his chest to prevent him from drawing her closer. "Nor am I forgetting that this building is crammed with busy people, any one of whom may decide he needs one or both of us for something."

His expression brightened. "You mean somebody could walk in and catch us in a compromising situation?"

"It crossed my mind."

"We're both over twenty-one," he reminded her.

"Yes, but I embarrass easily."

"You didn't seem embarrassed a while ago."

Alex wasn't about to tell him she'd been too rattled by her own response to feel anything else. "You aren't making this easy for me," she murmured.

Noah smiled faintly, but his gaze was intent. "I'm not making it easy for me either. In case you hadn't realized, sprite, I'm barely able to walk and talk at the same time when you're around."

"Be still my heart." It took all the control at Alex's

command to voice the flippant comment, and she wished she *could* order that organ to stop pounding so erratically.

"You don't believe me," he decided wryly.

"I haven't noticed you having any problems."

"That's because I'm being very macho. You know, laugh if it hurts, smile if it kills you."

Alex wanted to be flippant again. She wanted to laugh and change the subject and get herself off his lap before she lost her head and her heart. But it was too late and she knew it. She had already lost her heart, and her head held nothing but memories imperfectly remembered, memories with beginnings but no endings.

What ending would this memory have?

"Noah—"

"Blue-ribbon judging panel still out?"

She couldn't bear the half-shadowed look in his eyes or the taut steadiness of his voice. "No." Her hand rose of its own volition to touch his cheek. "No, the decision's in." She felt a muscle tense beneath her hand.

"Did we win?"

"We got—the blue." She heard her own voice break, her throat closing up.

Noah pulled her closer, one hand cradling the back of her head gently. She could feel a pulse throbbing in his throat and she snuggled even nearer, hiding her face because she was afraid of what he might have read in it.

"So we have . . . more than a beginning?" he asked.

Alex managed a shaky laugh. "That depends on you. I—I want more than a beginning." *I want a lifetime!* "More than just the moment."

He felt a jagged sense of relief that she was at least willing to try, at least sure he was important to her. But he couldn't help remembering she had told him once she wasn't looking for a ring and a promise.

He was important—but for how long?

Steadily he said, "Then we have more than a beginning. Because I want more too."

Ladders and paint buckets clattered loudly on the stairs outside the loft, and Alex smiled regretfully at him as she raised her head.

"Never the time and the place . . ." he muttered, as regretful as she.

Alex got to her feet, feeling again a wrenching sense of loss when she left his embrace. "You're spending a fortune to convert this building," she reminded him. "Those guys have to work. And so do I."

He stood, smiling. "I know. Well, the sooner we get to it, the sooner it's finished. Then there'll be time for us."

Six

The campsite was bare and empty, only the blackened pits of their fires remaining to give evidence of the Gypsies' stay.

He felt cold; emptiness ached in him. Gone. She was gone. Why? For the dear Lord's sake—why? Surely she had not put any credence in the jeering disbelief of her brothers? She could not have doubted he'd come back.

Obviously she *had* doubted.

With a muttered curse he turned and strode toward his waiting horse. He would find her. Somehow. If he had to search the world, he'd find her.

Noah woke with a start, his heart pounding and his chest hurting as though he had run a very great distance. He lay in the darkness of his bedroom and listened to the predawn silence, waiting for his pulse to slow and for the ache in his chest to ease.

It took a long time.

And he couldn't stop remembering the dream. It had been so vivid, so eerily real. He had felt pain and known the determination of a man driven to search for a Gypsy girl with green eyes.

Green eyes . . .

He linked his hands together behind his neck, staring up at the dim ceiling with a frown. He could remember another dream, one with soldiers and a blond woman, and himself wounded and hidden away in a musty barn. And now this odd dream, with himself another man in search of a Gypsy girl. It made no sense, he thought. Unless . . .

The instant a wild supposition crossed his mind, Noah rejected it. Dreams, he decided firmly, were merely the aimless ramblings of the subconscious. No more than that.

His decision made, a certain relief enabled Noah to turn over and try to go back to sleep. The present, he thought, was difficult enough to handle without additional problems from the past. Alex had as good as said he was important to her, that he mattered, but if anything, she seemed more elusive than ever.

And believing he was her "blue-ribbon affair" was, after all, no more than a belief. Alex could easily decide she had been mistaken, and vanish from his life. Noah was determined to prove to her that their relationship was indeed what both of them had wanted and needed, but he was worried that Cal's possible exposure would rob all of them of needed time.

He didn't want Alex to lose Cal. But, even more, he didn't want to lose Alex.

The work on the building had reached a critical point during the past several days—critical in more ways than one. The place was full of workmen; decisions were required of either Alex or Noah or both of them constantly, and Cal and Buddy had been shifted from one loft to another. The cats could safely remain in Alex's loft now since the workmen were finished there, but Theodora Suzanne Jessica Tyler had shown up without warning more than once, and Noah could feel the tension behind Alex's smiling façade.

Noah had said there would be time for them, and he hadn't pushed. They were always exhausted at day's end, content to share a meal and talk quietly for a while before turning in. He wanted more, needed more, but he was strongly aware that Alex required the peace of mind that only Cal's safety would give her. As for his own peace of mind . . .

He swore softly and pounded his pillow, closing his eyes. If only she would promise to stay.

It was a long time before Noah fell asleep, dreaming more peculiar dreams in which he was a stranger and a participant. This time there was a blond woman with green eyes in his arms, in an unfamiliar room before a roaring fire, and there was a blue uniform lying nearby on the floor. . . .

* * *

The wagon jolted and rattled, and the wavering image of the manor house was lost to sight behind the trees. She dashed a hand across her wet eyes, swearing in a weak imitation of her brothers. It served her right, they'd said, falling in love with an earl's son—the nobility loved easily and briefly, and a poor Gypsy girl would never be a countess. They had laughed and sneered, and shown her the gold he'd paid them to take her away.

And now she was going.

But she was leaving her heart behind with the man who had trampled it.

Alex pushed the dream out of her thoughts as she showered and got ready to face another day. It was just another depressing indication, she thought tiredly, of fate taking a cruel twist. The night before last she had watched a blue-clad soldier ride away from her in a dream, and last night she had seen the Gypsy girl abandoned.

She pulled on jeans and a light sweater, brushed her hair automatically and left it free around her face. She stared into her bedroom mirror for a long moment, looking into green eyes that were dark and anxious.

"You've lost him twice," she murmured to her reflection. "What makes you think you'll win this time? Third time lucky?"

Alex was hardly convinced that failure in the past automatically meant failure in the future, but she was worried. Fate seemed set against her in the person of an animal control officer and in the intrusive presence of a building full of workmen.

More than once during these past days Alex had wanted to throw herself at Noah and beg him to take her away somewhere. But this place had come to mean home because she was putting her mark on it and because he was here, and a part of her was unwilling to run away without first attempting to fight. She was torn between an urge to protect Cal at all costs and an ever-growing need for Noah.

She was sick with dread at the fear that she'd have to choose at some point between the man she loved and the lion she'd protected for more than six years.

And all at once it was just too much. A temper that the years had taught her—for the most part—to control snapped. Alex didn't like to not be in control of her life; she didn't like the feeling that she was half mad because she was remembering other lives; she didn't like being on guard and uneasy out of fear for Cal; and most of all—*most of all*—she was furious that circumstances had conspired to taunt her with her love for a man she just might have already lost twice.

Very steadily she walked into the living area of the loft, crossed to the couch, and bent to pick up a pillow.

*　　*　　*

When Noah hastily opened the door to Alex's loft, he wasn't quite sure what to expect. What met his incredulous, fascinated gaze, however, was a scene he would recall in later years with a grin.

Cal, his little white Buddy sitting trustfully between the great paws, lay sprawled on the carpeted platform, and both were observing their mistress with a comical serenity.

Noah didn't dare come in.

Pillows were flying across the room and pelting the wall near a stuffed and impervious polar bear, their quiet thumps going unheard amid the other sounds filling the loft. And it was those other sounds rather than the flying pillows that held Noah's attention.

Alex had not exaggerated her temper tantrums. Her tiny voice could never be roused to a shriek, he thought, but it was truly amazing how it had achieved the tone and general level of sound more commonly found among enraged dock workers. And she had borrowed the dock workers' vocabulary, along with a judicious sprinkling of furious truckers' swearing, and a wonderfully colorful mixture of curses most probably originating among sailors long at sea.

Then, quite abruptly, everything ceased. Alex shook her hair away from her face, took a deep breath, and gave Noah a very calm look. And her voice was utterly normal, unthreateningly tiny and sweet, when she said, "Want to help me pick up the pillows?"

"Is it safe?"

She chuckled softly, looking more relaxed than she'd been in days. "Of course. I wasn't mad at you." Crossing to begin to gather the pillows, she added thoughtfully, "I needed that."

Noah took a deep breath of his own, shut the door behind him, and came into the loft. "I apologize," he said. "I thought you were exaggerating."

"The tantrums?" Alex thrust a couple of pillows into his arms. "Oh, no, I wouldn't do that."

"I see you didn't."

Alex grinned faintly. "You look very wary."

"I'm just wondering," he said, "what set you off."

"No one thing. Just a general mad."

"Nothing to do with me?"

"I wouldn't say that. You might say I got mad partly because of you, but not *because* of you."

Noah carried the pillows to the couch, then turned to her with a frown. "Want to run that by me again?"

She dumped an armful of pillows beside his pile. "Well, you were part of why I was mad, but it wasn't anything you'd done."

"Was it something I didn't do?"

"No."

He stared at her. "Alex, at the risk of enraging you again—*why were you mad?*"

Alex wasn't about to confess her jumbled emotions. She settled for a relatively simple definition. "Fate. I was mad at fate."

"Why?"

She sat down among the pillows and gazed up at him. Well, she thought, why not? He probably knew exactly how she felt about him anyway. Mournfully, she said, "Fate has not been kind. Started out kind, mind you. Here I am in a new city, with a new life and a fairly new career. Then I met you, and that certainly looked like it was going to be a good thing."

"It didn't turn out that way?" he asked uneasily, sitting down on the coffee table to face her.

"That," she told him, "is where fate started to twist on me. It threw an animal control officer into the pot, along with assorted workmen just to keep things nicely crowded and confusing, and then other peculiar—things." She wasn't about to confess to insane dreams and speculations.

"What other things?"

"Just things. The point is," she added hastily, "that it all just got to be too much. And I got mad."

Noah was thoughtful, obviously trying to work his way through her explanation. Then, very carefully, he said, "Do I understand you to mean that you got mad because fate sort of dumped a group of quite un-necessary people between you and me?"

"How clearly you translate," she murmured. "Yes, that was the crux of the tantrum."

Gravely he said, "All you had to say was 'Noah, take me away from all this.' "

Alex didn't want to speculate on the similarity between his advice and the wistful thoughts she'd been harboring all week. Leaning forward to prop her elbows on her knees, she said, "Noah, take me away from all this."

"I'd love to," he said promptly.

She leaned back and gestured with a thumb toward their furry friends. "Them too?"

Noah sighed, "They are a problem, aren't they?"

"They certainly are. It's not easy—I speak from experience—to travel anywhere at all with a full-grown lion in tow. There is also the matter of the workmen; you and I are both needed until the work is completed. And just to add a bit of icing to the cake, if we did manage to sneak away somewhere, there would undoubtedly be suspicion in certain quarters."

"Teddy."

"The very same." Alex felt depression creeping over her again.

Noah was frowning slightly. "We could slip out at night," he said slowly. "Park your van at the door and get Cal into it unseen."

"And where would we go? Besides, the workmen—"

"Never mind the workmen." Noah's blue-gray eyes were bright. "Tell me, sprite, if neither of us was needed here, would you really want to go away with me for a while?"

Alex wavered for only an instant, thinking of two other loves she'd lost. Then she nodded steadily. "If we weren't needed. And if Cal were protected."

"He'll go with us," Noah said calmly.

"Go? Go where?"

"Away." Noah leaned forward. "Trust me?"

"Yes." It was an instinctive response.

His eyes were even brighter. "I'm glad."

"Yes, but, Noah—the workmen. Teddy."

"I've got a feeling we'll have to face Teddy sooner or later; why not postpone the inevitable and give ourselves time to think? As for the workmen, there's nothing easier—I'll just have them suspend the work until we return."

Alex blinked. "Return from where? How many places can you go for a visit *and* hide a lion?"

"I know of one place at least."

"Where? Noah—"

"I want it to be a surprise," he interrupted, but in a soothing tone of voice. "Just keep trusting me, okay? I'll talk to the men when they get here. You pack enough things for a week or two, and then we'll draw up a list of groceries for ourselves and the pets."

"Groceries?"

"Can't take a lion into a restaurant."

"True."

"Besides, there aren't any restaurants."

"There aren't any—"

"Get busy, sprite," he said cheerfully, rising to his feet as a clatter out in the hall announced the expected arrival of the workmen.

Alex sat there for a long moment, gazing after him. She was relieved at the thought of getting away for a while, with Cal out of harm's way at least temporarily. And she was torn between excitement and wariness at the thought of days of uninterrupted time with Noah.

She pushed the memory of dreams—or dreams of memory—aside, and let excitement win the tug-of-war.

* * *

"Hello."

Alex looked up from pulling a large suitcase through the door of her loft, and gave silent thanks that Cal was shut up in the bedroom. "Hi, Teddy."

"Kick me if I'm being nosy," the redhead said dryly, "but did Noah throw you out?"

Working on the principle that it was better to get over difficult fences as quickly and easily as possible, Alex aimed directly for this one. "Oh, no," she said happily. "As a matter of fact, he's so pleased with my work that he's giving me a little vacation. Isn't that nice?"

"Very. Going anyplace special?"

Alex said a silent good-bye to what was left of her virtuous reputation. "He hasn't told me yet. A surprise, he says."

"Oh, you're both going?"

"Uh-huh. For a week or so."

"Is the work on the building finished, then?" Teddy asked casually.

"Not quite. The workmen will finish it up when we get back."

There was a faint gleam of laughter in Teddy's brown eyes. "I see. And you're just the hired help?"

Alex managed to get all the dignity she could into a level stare at the other woman. "I started out that way," she said.

Teddy began to laugh. "Please don't be offended,

Alex—I think it's great. You two seem to belong together."

Sighing, Alex said, "We're in the process of working that out at the moment."

"Hence the vacation?"

"Something like that."

"Well, good luck to you both."

"Thanks."

Teddy started to turn back toward the door, then paused. "Oh—Alex, d'you think Noah would mind if I hung around and kept an eye on the place? I still haven't found my lion."

Alex made a mental note to remove every last *trace* of Cal's presence in the building. "I doubt it, but you'll have to ask him."

"Ask who what?" Noah asked as he came down the last few steps to Alex's side.

Teddy smiled at him. "Ask you if you'd mind me hanging around and keeping an eye on the place while you two are gone."

"Not at all," Noah said promptly.

"Thanks. Well, have fun, you two. I'll probably see you when you get back."

" 'Bye Teddy." Alex listened to Noah echo her good-bye, then she sank down on her suitcase. "D'you know what really irritates me, what makes me absolutely furious?" she asked him.

Noah studied her for a moment before deciding that there wouldn't be an explosion. "What?"

"I like her. I mean, I really like her."

He grinned a little. "Yeah, I know what you mean. It's like feeling friendly toward an IRS agent."

"Scary," she agreed, deadpan.

Noah looked down his nose at her. "Are you going to sit on that suitcase all day, sprite, or shall I take it out to the van?"

Alex got up. "Take it, by all means. By the way, when are we getting the groceries?"

"On the way."

"On the way *where*?"

He picked up the valise and started for the door. "Don't spoil my surprise," he told her over his shoulder.

Alex decided to give it up. She went back into the loft and began boxing up the baby food and cat food she'd stockpiled, knowing it would be easier to take what she had and just buy some extra when they got groceries. Besides, she thought, who knew where "on the way" might turn out to be? From the mysterious way Noah talked, it was the back of beyond at the very least—and possibly Mars.

Were there toothless lions or hungry kittens on Mars? Probably not, she decided, choking back a laugh. Or babies either, most likely. Which meant no baby food. She reminded herself to take along her blender in case Cal was forced to eat meals prepared from scratch. She heard Noah come into the loft, and turned to frown at him.

"Is there electricity on Mars?"

Noah took the question in stride. "Last I heard,

there weren't even little green men. Science dis-
proved them. Why?"

Alex sat down on a box and started laughing.
"Doesn't anything shake you?" she asked him finally.

"If you mean did I consider your question strange,"
he said affably, "the answer is yes. I trust you mean to
explain it."

"I was equating this mysterious place you're taking
me to with Mars," she explained.

"Ah. Now the question makes sense. Yes, there is
electricity there, but it's not the most dependable
since it orginates with an antique generator that only
works when it wants to. Do we need electricity?"

"For my blender. In case we run out of baby food for
Cal."

Noah leaned against the low partition and stared at
her. "If we run out," he told her, "we can always get
more. We can trade a few baubles to the savages."

"Very funny. You won't tell me where we're going,
after all."

"You told me yourself that the pioneers blazed a
trail across this country, and I'd guess there are a few
side trails as well; I don't think we'll get so far from
civilization that we'll fall off the edge of the world."

"And get eaten by dragons—I know, I know."

Noah was half-hiding a grin. "Well, you have to
admit the thought's a bit on the absurd side."

"For all I know," she said with dignity, "I'm being
kidnapped into white slavery. And along those lines,
I'd like to remind you that my lion would protect me
with every instinct his toothless self can lay claim to. I

would also like to inform you that lion-taming is not the *only* I learned how to do in the circus."

"Knife-throwing?" he queried with a look of mock uneasiness.

"Yes." She held up a finger in warning. "And my best friend was a Gypsy, so I can curse as well."

"You certainly can," he agreed, remembering the scene earlier that morning and choking back a laugh.

"That's not what I meant," she told him, reading his expression accurately.

"I meant to ask you where you learned some of those words," he said, persistent.

"Will you help me pack these?" she asked with a gesture toward the cans and jars lined up on the counter.

"If you'll answer my question."

Alex sighed. "I told you that the circus wasn't exactly Ringling Brothers; most of the people were a bit—rough. They'd been everywhere, and rarely did they go first class. After four years I picked up quite a few very impolite words. Satisfied?"

Noah began helping her pack the cans and jars. He was smiling, but he sent her a thoughtful look. "If these people were so rough—and I'll certainly take your word for that—then how did you survive four years with them? They . . . didn't hurt you or anything, did they?"

"No, they didn't hurt me." Alex smiled at him. "Even the worst of circus people have certain codes. I was one of them, so I was respected. Besides, my tough act didn't fool anybody; they knew I was a kid.

Instead of taking advantage of that, several of them taught me how to take care of myself."

"And I'll bet," Noah murmured, "they didn't teach you to fight by the Marquess of Queensberry's rules." He was torn between fascination and alarm by this revelation of her past.

Alex laughed. "Hardly. They advised survival and never mind manners or ethics."

He sat back on his heels and regarded her thoughtfully. "How did that mesh with the control you had to learn in order to train animals?" he asked, honestly interested.

She looked faintly surprised. "You know, I never thought about that. I suppose I was too young to realize it *shouldn't* mesh. I mean, nobody ever told me that learning to throw a man twice my weight over my shoulder was any different from staring down a lion without moving a muscle."

Noah began packing the jars and cans again, silent for a long moment. He was thinking of a sixteen-year-old kid filled with nothing but bravado and instinct, running away from an orphanage to join a circus. A kid with mental as well as physical strength, with the power to tame lions and toss men over her shoulder. A kid who had lived for four years among people with shadowy pasts and uncertain futures, and yet had emerged with a clear sense of herself and of what she wanted from life.

He wished he had known that kid, wished he could have watched a woman emerge from that willful, brave child's spirit.

"You're very quiet," Alex observed, gazing at him quizzically.

Noah was trying to build a mental picture of that girl's life. "Did you fly trapeze?" he asked. "You mentioned that to one of the workmen."

Alex looked both amused and puzzled. "Some. I learned the basics."

"What else?" When she lifted a brow at him, Noah smiled a little. "I'm just curious."

She shrugged. "Well, I tried most things. The teeterboard. High wire. Juggling and tumbling. I was even a clown a few times."

"A happy clown?"

"Sort of." Alex thought back a few years and smiled faintly. "A smile, but tears too. My Gypsy friend painted my face, I remember. She said it was apt."

"Did she ever read your palm?" he asked lightly.

"Oh, sure. She said—" Alex halted abruptly, remembering just exactly what the wizened old lady had said.

You're searching, child. You've always searched. You find him sometimes. Sometimes he finds you. Many partings, though. Much loss and pain. But happiness too. You'll find him again, child. A meeting in darkness, a stormy meeting, and another beginning.

"Alex?"

She looked at him for a moment, then conjured a teasing smile from somewhere. "She said I'd meet someone tall, dark, and handsome, of course."

Noah didn't believe that. Her face, he thought, had

held brief shock, and the green eyes had darkened. But he didn't probe.

A rational part of his mind didn't want to hear the answer.

Instead, he gave her an anxious look. "Have you met that guy yet, d'you think?"

"I am not about to pander to your ego." She closed the last of the boxes. "There, that's all done. Let's get them loaded into the van, all right?"

It was long after darkness had fallen before Alex's van pulled out into the street, its multicolored paint job obscured by night. Noah was at the wheel, while Alex sat in the bucket seat beside him and the two cats slept in the back with the luggage and boxes.

Alex was playing a guessing game.

"Why did we bring fishing rods?"

"Because we're going to fish."

"In a lake?"

"No. A stream."

"We're going east, right?"

"Unless we want to drive into the ocean."

"Funny. How far east are we going?"

"As the crow flies, about a hundred and seventy miles."

She reached into the glove compartment for a road map and a flashlight, then spent several minutes peering and measuring. "That puts us somewhere in the Sierra Nevada mountain range if we keep heading east," she decided.

"Spoil my surprise, why don't you?" he grumbled.

"We're going there?"

"If you *must* know—yes."

Alex swallowed a laugh at his disgruntled tone. "Well, I still don't know exactly where. All I know is that there are no restaurants, and there's a generator, and there's a stream. And, presumably, room for a lion."

"Definitely room for a lion."

She moved slightly and got a bit more comfortable. "Mmm. How long is this little trip going to take?"

"Hours. Which is one reason we brought along hot coffee."

"We can take turns driving," she offered.

"I'm the only one who knows where we're going," Noah pointed out.

There was a silence that consumed several miles, then Alex sighed. "This may be a bar to our future relationship," she said, "but I can't stand riding in a moving vehicle without talking to someone. Talk to me."

Noah started to laugh. "Who'd you talk to on the way out here?"

"Cal, of course. And if you don't talk to me, I'm going to crawl back there and wake him up."

"Don't disturb him. What shall we talk about?"

"Cabbages and kings."

Alex laughed. "Of course. The nonsense appealed to me."

"What else have you read, sprite?"

"Do we have to talk about me?" she complained. "I'm boring."

"Not to me, you aren't."

"You sweet talker you," she said, and smiled.

His grin flashed in the darkness. "I'm serious! I want to know everything about you, Alex. So start in the orphanage and work your way to now."

She was reluctant, but his obvious interest and his questions got her started talking. She told him about the years in the orphanage, choosing to talk about the good times and her own misbehavior, with its sometimes comical results. Unconsciously revealing her own pain, she mentioned friends who had been adopted and, therefore, left her life.

And she told him about the circus and her friends there. What it was like to perform in a cage full of half-tamed big cats, and to ride on the back of an elephant. Of tumbling as a clown and flying on the trapeze.

Somewhere during the telling she slipped easily into sleep, not noticing that Noah had silently used the automatic controls to recline her seat.

He turned on the radio, keeping the sound low in order not to disturb her. And he drove with the half-conscious, half-instinctive awareness of an expert driver, his mind focused mainly on her and what she'd told him.

And what she had revealed in the telling.

Seven

The sun was rising behind them when Alex stirred and sat up, yawning. She blinked at the new day, then turned to gaze at Noah's relaxed form behind the wheel. Then she looked through the windshield to find they were in the mountains and everything was dawn-colored and beautiful.

"Good Lord, I've slept through the trip," she murmured.

"So you have." He sent her a smile. "As a matter of fact, you've been lousy company. Mind getting the coffee? It's on your side."

Alex fumbled to bring her seat upright, then reached for the thermos. "Why didn't you wake me? You must have needed coffee hours ago."

"I managed." Accepting the cup she held out, he

was able to cope one-handed with the winding road. "Thanks."

She found a collapsible cup in the glove compartment and poured coffee for herself before capping the thermos again. Unusually reluctant to completely wake up and face the day, she yawned once more and peered at the winding road ahead. Dreams, she thought dimly. But this time the dreams had been a crazy kind of split-screen image, half-showing a blond woman gazing at an empty, dusty road, and half-showing a crying Gypsy girl in a jolting wagon.

Alex shook away the memory as Noah spoke, concentrating on what he was saying to her.

"We'll be there in about an hour. The cabin is miles from anything or anyone, so Cal won't have to stay inside all the time. That is, unless— He won't wander off, will he?"

"No, he'll stay close. Whose cabin is it?"

"Belongs to a friend of mine. I did some work for him a while back, and he said I could use the cabin whenever I liked. I called him yesterday, and he said he wasn't going back up there until fall."

"We staying that long?" Alex asked politely, beginning to wake up.

"It crossed my mind," Noah answered. "We could abandon the world."

"No, we couldn't," she said suddenly. "I just remembered—we didn't get groceries. We'll starve if we abandon the world."

He chuckled. "We got groceries. Or, rather, I did. You slept right through it. I found an all-night grocery store, locked up the van, and brought the stuff out and loaded it. You slept."

Alex stared at him. "I didn't realize I was so tired."

Noah sent her a look that was warm and gentle. "I don't think it was just tiredness, sprite. You've been tense ever since Teddy showed up."

She thought about that. Yes, she'd been tense, and she hadn't slept well since Cal's safety had been threatened. But being with Noah had made her feel protected. She had never in her life looked to anyone else for protection; the fact that she'd apparently accepted it from Noah was—well, just another confirmation.

How long had she loved this man?

They reached the cabin an hour later after following a winding dirt road that was scarcely more than a trail into an unspoiled wilderness. The little trail stopped beside a cabin on the edge of a clear stream. Mountains towered all around; the cabin and the stream were situated in a narrow valley that was itself far above sea level, and nothing else built by man could be seen.

Alex didn't realize she was holding her breath until Noah came around the van to stand beside her. Then she looked up at him happily. "It's beautiful!"

Noah could have echoed the comment, but he wouldn't have been talking about the view or the rustic log cabin. He would have meant something far more human and heart-catchingly appealing. The sleepless night had left his willpower dangerously low and his instincts just barely above surface level; he had to clear his throat before he could speak.

"Why don't we let the pets out and then unload the van?" he suggested.

She agreed cheerfully, going around to the rear of the van and swinging open the double doors. Cal waited patiently while they shifted aside grocery boxes, the kitten sitting with equal patience between his front paws.

"That kitten's weird," Noah commented as he set two boxes outside on the ground.

"No, he isn't," Alex defended the little creature, unconsciously proving the force of Noah's belief when she lifted the kitten and then set him casually in Cal's thick mane once the lion was on the ground.

"Oh, no?" Noah gazed pointedly at the picture of a lion wandering around the clearing with a tiny white kitten perched easily between its round ears.

Alex followed his look and then laughed. "I suppose he is a little strange at that."

Noah watched the kitten's expertise in maintaining his balance on his large mount, then shook his head in bemusement as he followed Alex into the cabin.

Within moments Alex had decided that although Noah's friend had obviously wanted a rustic vacation cabin, he also liked his comfort. The cabin was large and beautifully kept, outside as well as in. The interior consisted of three large rooms: two bedrooms and a large combination living/dining area with a spotless kitchen, and a completely modern and functional bathroom. The decoration was plain but comfortable, with sturdy furniture and wear-resistant fabrics in warm brown and rust tones. And there was a huge river-rock fireplace that promised warmth even if the generator-powered baseboard heaters failed.

Alex was more than tempted to abandon the world.

They settled in quickly, leaving the front door open to allow Cal to wander in and out while they unpacked and put away provisions. Noah started the generator, which gave them lights and power. Then Alex fixed breakfast and fed the pets. She refused Noah's offer to help in cleaning up, ordering him instead to go to bed and catch up on lost sleep.

"I'm fine," he objected. "A shower and shave and I'll be as good as new."

"You're punchy," she told him firmly. "You nearly tripped over Cal a minute ago, and if you can't see something *that* big, you need sleep!"

He grinned. "All right, so losing sleep affects me."

"It's nice to know you're not perfect," she muttered, scraping plates at the sink.

"You mean I am *nearly* perfect?"

"Go to bed."

"I suppose I can't persuade you to come with me?"

"Noah!"

"Okay, okay. Don't wander off while I'm asleep, will you?"

"Wouldn't think of it."

Alex worked contentedly, listening to Cal grumble

softly at the kitten attacking his whiskers and feeling relaxed and almost at peace.

Not completely at peace because she was still wary at the thought of beginnings with uncertain and potentially painful endings. Still, she knew the beginning to be behind them, and that in itself was a commitment to follow through to whatever lay ahead.

And she knew, too, that her agreement to accompany Noah up here was also a tacit agreement that it was time their relationship progressed.

Alex had virtually skipped an important part of a girl's life; she had left childhood behind one night when she'd hidden herself in the railroad cars of a departing circus. She had never tested her wings in the normal fashion of teenage girls, never sat beside a boy in a beat-up car and waited breathlessly for a first kiss. Her first kiss had come to a woman, assured by years of handling dangerous animals and potentially dangerous people.

She had never dated in her teens and only infrequently since then and, as she'd told Noah, no one had waved a blue ribbon at her.

Until him.

The blue ribbon was between them now, acknowledged for what it was. More than a beginning.

Alex was testing her wings at twenty-six, but she more than half-believed she had flown before . . . with this man. Her only certainty was that she loved him and needed him.

She didn't know what Noah felt, except for desire. He cared for her, she knew; the warmth in his eyes was more than passion, more than simple need. Her instincts told her he was not a man who cared lightly or incautiously. Knowledge of him these last weeks told her he was an honest man, an intelligent and humorous man.

Old memories—or dreams—told her even more. A soldier had gazed at her with gray-blue eyes reflecting the quiet dignity and weary devastation of a man who hated war, but fought. A man who loved. And the son of an earl had looked at her with the incredulous tenderness of a man grasping heaven against all odds.

But they had left her. One had gone back to his hated war. One had paid gold to be rid of her.

Restless, Alex fixed herself a cup of coffee and went to sit on the top step just outside the open front door of the cabin. Cal and Buddy came outside to sprawl on the porch, sleepy and peaceful in the warmth of the day.

She gazed off but looked inward, ignoring the view. She wanted to convince herself that those past "lives" she "remembered" held no real meaning, no connection to herself or this life. She wanted to believe that they were no more than bizarre instances of a creative subconscious, somehow triggered to spin tales in dream.

She couldn't convince herself.

Shifting her cup to her left hand, Alex stared down at her right palm for a moment. She shook her head slightly, willing the line to change, or her memory of another palm to fade. She had had only a glimpse of that other hand, after all, and perhaps . . . No. She remembered.

Alex sighed and once more turned a blind gaze to the view. For the first time she felt certainty. Mad she might very well be, but she believed she had lived at least twice before. And twice before she had loved Noah.

And lost him.

She frowned. Once he had returned to a hated war, leaving her to stare down an empty, dusty road. Then there was that other man, the one who had paid to be rid of her. Or . . . had he? Alex could vividly remember those gray-blue eyes looking at her with something very like adoration; would that man have paid her brothers to take her away?

It didn't ring true somehow, and yet she had no way of knowing. Unless and until her wayward memory told her how the stories ended.

Alex badly wanted to know. She thought of two adages, only one of which was slightly comforting: the third time's the charm; three strikes . . . and you're out. And how could she know this was indeed the third time? She wondered if her entire history was a series of lives during which she had lost the same man.

She felt her shoulders stiffening in determination. All right, then. Maybe she *had* lost. But that didn't mean she had to lose again. She had learned a kind of strength few women ever knew—the strength to master and control wild animals. If she could stare a tiger down, she could certainly look fate in the eye.

She might even throw a saddle on the beast and tame it.

"There's that whip and chair."

At the sound of Noah's soft voice Alex looked around quickly and felt a curious lurch of her heart. He was standing in the doorway watching her, and the flesh-and-blood reality of him made her even more determined.

She wouldn't lose him.

Not again.

"I wasn't even out here," Noah complained.

Alex got to her feet and set the empty coffee cup on the railing that enclosed the porch. "I wasn't waving them at you," she said mildly.

"Oh? Who, then?"

"Not who. What." Alex took three steps and slid her arms around his waist, smiling up at him. "Fate."

Instantly his arms went around her, and his answering smile was both whimsical and bemused. His eyes were bright. "Fate. And to what do I owe this newly affectionate sprite? Fate again?"

"Let's call it a disagreement with fate."

"Ah." Noah grinned down at her. "Alex, that makes no sense at all. But I'm not complaining. I'd shake hands with the devil if he'd promise to make you smile at me like that again."

Unconsciously Alex smiled again—like that. "No need to sell your soul. I'm not cheap, but I don't cost that much."

His smile faded, and his eyes darkened suddenly. "Don't you?" he murmured. "Well, I'm like that man who found a pearl beyond price; I'd sell everything I have for you."

Alex had never realized that love could be declared without the word itself, but she realized it then. And the breath caught in her throat. She stood on tiptoe even as his head bent, her lips meeting his fiercely, tenderly.

Noah's arms tightened around her as something exploded, a detonation as raw and powerful as a solar flare. It was a savage release, a wild abandon tempered only by love, its sharp edges smoothed but its force undiminished.

His lips slanted hungrily across hers, taking what she offered with a need very nearly intolerable in its yearning torment. The weeks of patience had banked an essential fire, and it burst its bounds hotly. The slender body pressed against his fed the fire, built it into a flame that engulfed them both.

Alex thought she cried out when his lips left hers, a cry that was older than any memory could ever be and aching with emotions spiraling out of control. Her arms went up around his neck as he lifted her into his arms, and she felt a fierce eagerness that surprised her mind, but didn't surprise her heart. She knew he was carrying her through the cabin to his bedroom, but her gaze was fixed on his lean face and she saw only gray-blue eyes shot with silvery flames.

"The whip and chair won't help you this time," he said huskily, kicking the bedroom door shut behind them and setting her gently on her feet by the bed. "I've found my lioness . . . and she is mine."

"Maybe you're hers," Alex whispered, giddily aware that his hair was still damp from a shower, that he bore an herbal scent like a rainwashed forest in the spring.

"Promise?" Noah asked, his lips feathering over her cheek and down her throat as Alex tipped her head back. His hands slid to her shoulders, probing gently, and then he was slowly parting the buttons of her blouse.

Alex couldn't force an answer past the pounding lump in her throat. Dizzy, she closed her eyes, feeling her pulse racing and her body quivering. A part of her mind was aware that her own hands had risen to cope with the buttons of his shirt, the movements as natural and familiar as if this were something she had always done. His shirt fell away as he shrugged, and hers followed a moment later. Alex kicked her shoes away without thought, her eyes drifting open when she felt the lacy bra smoothed away by his hands.

She found herself gazing into eyes that evoked a wrenching surge of emotion from deep inside of her. For a flashing instant she was looking into other gray-blue eyes in strange yet familiar faces, and her body told her they belonged to him.

She might have cried out again, but Alex didn't know and didn't care if she had. She knew only that familiar hands, hers and his, rid them both of clothing that was a barrier between them. The bed was soft beneath her, and the afternoon sun slanted through the window to cast a glow in the cool room.

"Alex . . ." His voice was hoarse, driven, but the hands touching her were achingly gentle. "God, you're so lovely!"

Her fingers bit into his shoulders and a moan lodged somewhere within her as he stroked and shaped her quivering flesh. Eyes half-closed, she watched his absorbed face, a sense of wonder filling her: there was a tremor in his hands because of her, and she was incredulous that she could affect him so. Then his lips found the pointed need of her breast, and she heard the soft, wild cry that escaped her throat.

He seemed to be starving for her, for the touch and taste of her, and Alex felt the hot, restless ache building intolerably within her. Her shaking hands moved to touch his back, fingers tracing the rippling muscles and the clean line of his spine. Then she was holding his shoulders again as his caresses slid lower, tension spiraling until she could barely be still. Every touch of his mouth caused heat to radiate outward, the tiny wildfires spreading until she was aflame and the burning was a sweet, breathless agony.

"Noah . . ."

He murmured something inaudible against her flesh, soothing and stirring, his lips tormenting her striving body. Alex was only barely aware of anything but his touch and her own building need, but what she was aware of was an elusive, purely feminine realization. Noah had a strength and power she could never overcome, because he was stronger and she knew it. But she had a power all her own, and her determination to hold this man set alight instincts older than memory.

She could tame a beast; it remained to be seen if she could also tame the beast in a man.

Acting purely on instinct and rampaging need, her body moved against his hot, taut flesh. Her fingers shaped his lean ribs as he rose above her, and her limbs moved to cradle him, imprison him. She caught him, a beloved thief, giving as he took, taking as he gave, holding him as only a woman could hold a man.

They were old lovers rather than new, moving in sync as if in a dance practiced through the ages. Green eyes and blue-gray locked together in an infinite shaft of time's light, a moment stretching into forever. A fire crackled in a stone hearth and a stream rushed past a mossy glade . . . and a dozen other realities fused into a single blinding instant that rocked their universe . . . voices that were barely human crying out in the sweet devastation of a tiny death. . . .

Alex didn't know or care how much of the day had passed, but a part of her noted that the sun's glow had faded. It was cool and dim in the bedroom, silent now, and utterly peaceful. She knew that a sheet covered their bodies, but her senses were tuned only to the touch of flesh on flesh. His shoulder pillowed her head in surprising comfort, and his arms held her in an embrace that made her feel a cherished thing.

"Know what?" she asked.

"What?" His arms tightened, and his voice was as hushed as hers.

Smiling a little, she said, "You're the best afternoon I've ever spent."

Noah chuckled softly. "I'm glad. You're my best year—and more."

Alex managed to raise herself on an elbow, and gazed down at him with a lifted brow. "Coming from a man who's several times gotten his feet wet, that's quite a compliment. I think."

"Bet on it." His voice matched hers in lightness, but the gray-blue eyes were curiously stormy. "You're quite a lady, Stephanie Alexandra Cortney Bennet."

She smiled slowly. "Ladies don't carry whips and chairs," she reminded him. "Or attack men in the middle of the afternoon."

"Was that an attack?" he mused. "I seem to remember doing a bit of roaring myself."

"That was a by-product of my attack," she told him solemnly.

"I don't get any credit?"

Alex looked at him for a long moment, and her intentional lightness faded away. "My best year," she said almost harshly. "And more."

Noah waited, his eyes holding hers, wondering if she could hear or feel his heart pounding.

Her hand moved to touch his cheek, and she felt that harshness in her throat, the harshness of her determination to fight fate. "You get credit for that." She was afraid, afraid to let go and love. Afraid of endings. But more afraid of losing . . . again. "I—I've never said it before," she choked.

"Said what?" His voice rasped. "What, Alex?"

She was caught by the storm in his eyes, something within her rising to match its force, and the fear lost out to certain knowledge. "I've never said I love you. But I do, Noah. I love you."

The storm turned to silver, and he pulled her head down gently to kiss her with a savage tenderness. "Sprite, my sprite," he murmured hoarsely, his eyes so bright they warmed her anxious soul. "God, how I love you! You've haunted my days and nights since I heard your voice in the darkness. . . ."

There was a moment of vertigo, and Alex was looking up at him, filled with the ridiculous conviction that she was smiling all over. Not that she cared. Loving and being loved was all that mattered, and her bottled hurricane certainly had a way of loving that was impossible to resist.

To say the least.

"Noah!"

"Yes, darling sprite?"

"If you don't give me back that robe, I'll burn supper!"

"Forest sprites never wear clothes," he said firmly.

"I'm not a nudist! Give it back—Cal's watching!"

"No, he isn't. He very tactfully averted his eyes. I saw him."

Alex unconsciously played her sprite role to the hilt

when she placed her hands on her hips and glared at him. Her long blond curls flowed around her shoulders, and the rest of her was covered only in a golden tan.

Noah dropped the robe and lunged at her.

Warding him off with a long-handled wooden spoon, she managed to slip past and grab her robe. The fact that she also managed to get it on before he could steal it again spoke volumes for her dexterity.

"Spoilsport," he grumbled.

"You're a horrible man. Worse, you're a *sneaky*, horrible man!"

"But you love me?"

"For my sins." She twisted adroitly. "And get your hands off that sash!"

In a reasonable tone Noah said, "We're all alone up here. There aren't any people for *miles*. We came up here to relax and unwind."

"I can do that dressed, thank you." Alex stuck her nose in the air and turned back to the stove.

Noah slid his arms around her from behind. He kept his hands off the sash.

"How," she started to say, "am I supposed to cook when you do that?"

"Am I getting to you?" he asked hopefully, nuzzling her neck.

Alex actually managed to keep her voice steady without first clearing her throat. "What you're doing is making me burn supper. Stop *roaring*!"

"Lion can't mute his roar," Noah said.

Attempting to transfer the contents of a pot into a

dish, Alex almost roared herself. "D'you want to eat this or wear it?" she demanded.

He sighed and released her. "I knew it," he mourned. "This afternoon you were in the mood for a mind-blowing, teeth-rattling, heart-stopping, eye-rolling fling. It was just a temporary urge for my body, wasn't it?"

Alex set the empty pot into the sink and then turned to face him, leaning against the counter. Holding laughter strictly at bay, she infused her voice with polite incredulity. "A temporary urge for what?"

"My body," he prompted her, undaunted.

She studied the robed body in question from black hair to bare feet, then lifted her brows in gentle disbelief.

Noah's suddenly crestfallen expression was belied by laughing eyes. "It wasn't an urge for my body?"

"I didn't get my teeth rattled," she said.

"Oh."

Alex burst out laughing, but still managed to evade Noah when he lunged again. "Oh, no! You have to eat to keep up your strength; I'm determined to get my teeth rattled."

"Witch!"

"I thought I was a sprite."

They watched night come over the tiny valley, building a fire in the river-rock fireplace to ward off the chill. Light teasing was the rule, but there were exceptions scattered here and there that rekindled their need as if it had never been sated.

It was still early when Noah began to bank the fire, and Alex headed for their bedroom, her heart beating in her throat and her body warm from within. She turned down the corners and climbed into bed after shedding the robe, smiling to herself. But her smile became suddenly half worried and half rueful when a four-hundred-pound lion climbed up beside her, carrying a trusting white kitten in his mouth.

Alex watched Cal release Buddy, watched the kitten curl up between the broad forepaws of his friend. And she sighed. She looked up to see Noah standing in the doorway, and shrugged helplessly.

"He's used to sleeping with me."

Noah held the door and looked Cal straight in the eye. "Out, pal," he said pleasantly. "There's not room enough for both of us."

She started to warn him that it was unwise to stare any lion in the eye, even gentle Cal. But something, a newer instinct, held the warning unsaid. Instead, she waited silently, looking from the lion to the man. A part of her was somehow aware that this was a purely male matter, a curiously decisive, silent battle that would need to be settled only once.

And it was.

Returning the stare for a long moment, it was Cal who gave in. He picked his Buddy up and climbed off the bed. And he butted Noah's thigh gently as he passed by him and left the room.

Calmly Noah closed the door and came to join Alex in the bed.

"Very impressive," she commented.

His eyes gleamed at her. "Not at all. Just a question of who got the lioness."

Her arms slid around his neck as he reached for her. "Oh? Well, there's more than one way to tame a lion. . . ."

She watched the dusty road. For weeks now she had watched. She offered water and what food she had to the weary soldiers making their way back south. She bandaged old wounds and answered eager questions about the whereabouts of the families in the area.

She searched faces.

Most wore gray, but there were some in blue. The war had split families, tearing more than a country down the middle. Of the blue-clad men she asked hesitant questions.

They had no answers for her.

The war was ended. A tattered, bloody South defeated. She had known, in the beginning, that it would be so. She had lost everything in a hopeless cause. Her father, brothers.

Now . . . him.

Her heart told her he lived. He was safe. Her mind told her he would not return to her.

More weeks passed. The road became even more empty. Fewer soldiers came by her gate. She waited and watched. At night she lay before the stone fireplace and remembered strong arms and gray-blue eyes.

Until, finally, she turned away from the road, and

the memories. But not fully. A part of him lived within her.

She called on strength earned in the battle to survive, and began to repair her war-ravaged land. Her home. There were no tears left.

Alex woke to find tears on her cheeks. She wiped them away, careful not to disturb Noah. His warmth helped ease the coldness inside of her, and she moved yet nearer to his body. His arms tightened around her even in sleep, and Alex relaxed in his embrace.

But she stared into the darkness a very long time before sleep would return, one hand resting on her flat stomach.

Eight

"Shall we fling?"

"Not without music," she answered.

"Darling sprite, we'll make our own music."

"You're still trying to rattle my teeth, aren't you?"

"It's a question of masculine pride."

"I'll dance at the wake."

"What're we burying?"

"Your masculine pride."

Noah sighed. "A guy could get hurt in the cross-fire," he observed in a cowed tone.

"You started the shooting."

"I just asked a simple question."

"And I answered it. I never fling in the woods." Alex removed Buddy from Cal's mouth and set him down on the blanket they had spread in a clearing by the stream. "You were going to fish," she reminded Noah, "and I was going to read. Those plans still sound good to me." She picked up her book and leaned back against Cal, using his willing side for a pillow.

Noah sighed again and bent down to gather his fishing rod and tackle box. "You should have told me you didn't enjoy fishing," he told her.

"You didn't ask. Is it going to be a bar to our future relationship?"

"I shouldn't think so. As long as you don't object to my fishing." Noah kept his voice light, his heart leaping as always whenever she casually mentioned a future for them.

"I don't object a bit," she said firmly.

He straightened and gazed down at her in silence for a moment, wondering for a countless time if he dared ask her to commit herself to him. And, for a countless time, he shied away from that.

They had spent days alone but for the pets, days of peace and laughter and passion. In some ways Noah felt secure in her love, and yet there was still something elusive about her. "I love you" was still not an easy thing for her to say, yet she said it often. She was clearly more comfortable now with touching and being touched, quick to reach out to him or respond to him.

Yet he had awakened several nights to find her awake, still and silent beside him in their bed. To his concerned questions she inevitably replied that it had been "just a nightmare" and seemed so unwilling to talk about it that he hadn't pressed her for details.

"You're not fishing," Alex murmured, looking up at him over the top of her book.

Noah pushed the troubling thoughts aside. "Actually, I am," he told her. "I'm using my sexy body for bait and hoping to catch you."

"You're insatiable."

"Oh, you noticed that?"

"Noticed?" Alex rested the book against her raised knees and stared at him. "Noticed?" she repeated in rising incredulity.

"You should be flattered."

She cleared her throat in a rather pointed way and lifted the book again.

"Can I help it," Noah demanded aggrievedly, "if I'm at the mercy of this violent passion you've roused in me? Can I help it if I have to grab you every time you walk by?"

"Go fish," she told him.

"I'd rather catch you," he said wistfully.

Alex didn't take the bait.

After a moment, sighing mournfully, Noah made his way to the edge of the stream. He eyed the water, then walked a few yards farther upstream before choosing a spot. But before he could even bait his hook, arms slid around him from behind.

"You caught me," Alex said breathlessly. "I just can't resist your sexy body!"

Noah dropped everything.

He could feel her gaze on him as he saddled the

horse, and knew without looking what expressions those green depths would hold. No condemnation, no censure, no recriminations. Only quiet strength and a softness that was wistful because a war had robbed her world of softness.

She was a lady.

She wouldn't ask him to stay, he knew. It was not in her, this gentle and gracious woman, to put herself between him and his duty. She had hidden him, tended and healed his wounds. She had fed more than his body, her beauty and gentle touch a salve to his weary spirit.

She had shared with him her own weary soul . . . and her bed. Held him in the night as he had held her, with a passion as violent and overpowering as a summer storm.

And now he was leaving her.

Alone, but for a handful of loyal servants. Alone in a war-torn land. Alone amid the shattered remains of what had been her life.

He led the horse from the barn, aware of her soft footsteps behind him. He swung into the saddle, arranged the reins methodically. If he looked at her, he knew, if he gazed into those quiet eyes, he was lost. He was, he realized dimly, lost anyway, because he was about to leave the only anchor he had found in this hated war. The only reality.

And the only person he had ever loved.

"Thank you." Abrupt. Brutal.

"Take care." Her quiet, gentle response.

Shoulders stiff. he rode blindly down the dusty road.

Noah woke. cold and shivering. desolate. He had released Alex sometime during the night. and now gently gathered her sleeping body close again.

It was a long time before he felt warm.

He wasn't a man who had ever thought seriously about impossible things. Analytical for the most part. he considered to be real what he could see or touch. Yet Noah had more than once photographed things he had not consciously seen. capturing a moment or a fleeting expression he could not have reasonably anticipated.

Luck he called it.

But as the days passed. Noah began to wonder more and more often if there were realities that couldn't be touched. but only felt and believed. He wondered because his analytical mind had begun to add things up. Just flashes. Dreams. Curious. out-of-sync moments. Feelings.

Feelings from other times.

He dreamed almost every night now. usually two separate dreams. One always involved a union soldier and a woman with blond hair and green eyes who had hidden him. healed his wound. and loved him. The other always concerned a raven-haired Gypsy girl with wild green eyes and a man who adored her.

Noah had dismissed the dreams as the erratic ramblings of his subconscious at first. But a pattern had formed, and there was nothing erratic or rambling about that. The dreams were *serial.* They had progressed, from instance to instance, each dream continuing to tell a clear and coherent story.

A lord's son had watched a Gypsy girl dance before a bonfire, her green eyes beckoning, her smile teasing. Meetings followed, secret and secluded, because her family thought little of nobility and his thought even less of Gypsies. Words of love were the sounds of two hearts beating together, desire a pagan song celebrated beneath the trees. They loved and planned. And when he had to leave the countryside on business for his father, he promised to return. And he had returned . . . to find her gone.

And a wounded union soldier had found help and solace from a gentle Southern lady who hid him within her home. She had nursed him, fed him. Asking nothing in return, she provided a haven where his weary body and spirit could rest. She was the one spot of gracious beauty in his life, and he loved her. Loved her in a bed where generations of her family had come into the world. Loved her before a crackling fire in an old stone fireplace. Loved her with the desperation of a man about to return to war. And then he left her.

Dreams. Or . . . dreams of memories.

Memories of dreams?

He didn't know.

Often Noah caught himself looking in Alex's eyes for something. The wild spirit of a Gypsy girl. The quiet strength and gentleness of a woman risking her own safety for his. And shaken, he often found one or both of the qualities he sought in the depths of her green eyes.

Enchanted green sirens, wild and fey, sometimes beckoned to him when he teased or she teased, prompting a flashing image in his mind of black hair and a cool forest glade. Lovemaking by a rushing stream. And in quiet moments her green eyes were soft and wistful, and he could almost smell the musty disuse of an old barn and see dust hanging heavy in the summer air. See a once-gracious house pitted and scarred by a vicious war. Feel the satiny softness of smooth skin reflecting a fire's golden glow.

He could remember waking from a vague dream to hear a voice, familiar yet strange, speaking words that had made no sense. Then.

Oh, see! Our lifelines match! We are bonded, my love. Fated to share all our lives together!

Noah didn't believe in impossible things. But his perception of what was, in fact, possible was beginning to change.

There was so much about Alex that was familiar to him! Tiny things such as gestures or tricks of expression, and larger things—the way her slender body felt in his arms. Familiar. And so right.

How long had he loved her?

Insane, he thought. *I'm insane. I love her so much I'm looking for ties stretching beyond the both of us, for anything that will bind us together.*

He didn't dare confide the wild suppositions to Alex. She'd think he was stark raving mad!

*   *   *

"We haven't come up with a way to save Cal from Teddy's clutches," Alex reminded him one night as they cuddled together on the couch in front of the fireplace.

"That worries you a lot, doesn't it?" he asked quietly.

Alex, her determination to hold on to this man strengthened during the past days, silently fought off panic at the thought of having to choose between the two lions in her life. "It worries me," she admitted. "Before, I would have just—taken Cal away. Moved on."

"Before me?"

She nodded, gazing into the fire. "It never bothered me much. Pulling up stakes, I mean. I never regretted that."

"But you would this time?"

"Of course I would."

"Why?" he asked softly, his voice husky.

Alex felt a gathering tension, uneasily aware of a matching tension filling Noah's lean body. It was suddenly difficult to breathe, and she had the strong impression that they were at a fork in the road. Something had to be resolved between them, and she was afraid, desperately afraid, that she would somehow lose him again.

She couldn't lose him again.

"Why, Alex?"

"Because . . . I love you."

He was silent and still for such a long time that Alex's control broke. She jumped to her feet, pacing over to the open door and staring out into the night. In a voice that was strange to her ears, she said, "I used to believe that life was very simple. I got that from the animals, I suppose. They—animals—aren't much concerned with tomorrow. They live day to day. I've always been that way. When I didn't like my life anymore, I changed it in some way. I don't think I ever learned to stand and fight."

"Alex—"

She barely heard him. "There was never anything I wanted to fight for. To join the circus I ran away. To protect Cal I ran away. It's very easy to get into the habit of running. And the worst thing about running isn't just that it's cowardly. The worst thing is that it doesn't solve the problem. It's like being on a merry-go-round; eventually you come back to where you started."

"Alex—"

His voice was nearer, just behind her, but Alex kept talking in that strange voice. "I've reached that point now. I want to change my life again. I could change it by running. Again. I could change it by staying. If I run, I know what I'll lose. If I stay, I don't know if I can *win.*"

"You want to win safety for Cal?" he asked quietly.

"That's part of it. A large part." She stared out into the darkness. "Part of it is something I—I need to win for myself."

"What do you need for yourself?"

Alex gestured almost helplessly, trying to find words. "Maybe a place. Or a kind of certainty. No more running, I guess." She turned suddenly, leaning back against the doorjamb and staring up at him. "I used to watch old Western movies in the orphanage. D'you know what I always looked for, waited for in those movies?"

"What?"

"The part where the good guys made a stand. It always happened. They'd build barricades around a town or a ranch, and they'd fight it out. They were *protecting* something. Something worth standing and fighting for. And whenever the movie reached that point, I always knew the good guys were going to win."

"Because they had a place to fight?"

"I suppose."

"And that's what you want now?" Noah asked. "A place to fight?"

Alex gazed up at him. "A place to fight. A reason to stand and fight. It'd be easier to run, Noah."

His hands rose to rest on her shoulders. "Honey, I can't promise that by staying you'll keep Cal safe forever. I can't even promise he'll be safe for a week or a month. I *can* promise that I'll do everything in my power to help you keep him safe. And I can promise you a place to fight. As for a reason to stand . . ." He took a deep breath. "I love you. I hope that's reason enough."

A fork in the road. Alex had chosen, she knew, long before.

She smiled slowly. "I think it's time I stopped fading into the misty night."

Noah sighed an eternity's pent-up breath. It was a commitment of sorts, and more than he'd dared hope for. Unwilling to touch what was fragile in its newness, he reached for lightness. "It's about time!" he reproved her sternly. "I was beginning to think I'd perjured myself for nothing."

"Perjured yourself?"

"The scarred trees at home. I invented kids with hatchets, remember?"

"So you did." Alex let her arms circle his waist. "But you said Teddy didn't believe you."

"That doesn't change the fact that I lied."

"My hero."

Gravely Noah said, "A man's gotta do what a man's gotta do."

Alex giggled. "All you need are six-guns and a ten-gallon hat!"

"Would you please," Noah requested politely, "allow me to enjoy my heroism for just a few moments?"

"All right, stranger. But tell me something, will you?"

"Yes, ma'am?"

"When the bad guys bite the dust, are you going to kiss me or your horse?"

"In the grand tradition of Western epics . . ." he began grandly.

"Yes?"

"I'll kiss you, of course."

"Gee, you mean I beat out Trigger?"

"By a nose."

She choked. "That's terrible!"

"But honest."

Releasing him, Alex ducked under his arm and went back to sit on the couch. "If you'll please stop playing with words," she said briskly, "we can discuss strategy."

Noah joined her, grinning. "If you insist. But I was having fun playing with words."

Alex eyed him thoughtfully. "How did you ever manage to get so big without growing up?"

"Eating spinach," Noah replied promptly.

She put her head in her hands briefly, then cleared her throat as she glared at him. "Strategy."

"Yes, ma'am. Well, as I see it, we have two basic alternatives. One, we go on hiding a four-hundred-pound lion to the best of our combined abilities. Two, we somehow manage to make an illegality legal and let Cal go public."

Alex winced. "Lousy options," she commented darkly.

"There are drawbacks to both," he agreed. "You've been lucky for six years, but lady luck's a fickle creature. I don't think we'd better count on luck to keep him safe. That means we'll have to be very, very careful. As for the second alternative, we'll have to be very sure we *can* make Cal legal before we—so to speak—let the cat out of the bag."

"I knew you wouldn't be able to resist saying that."

"No applause for my wit?"

"We're going to bury your wit along with your masculine pride."

"There's no need for that," he said on a sigh. "Both are already gone where you're concerned. I have the wit of a ten-year-old—"

"He admits it."

"—and my pride is in my shoes."

"I thought we were talking about Cal."

"No, we're talking about the other lion in your life."

"Let's save one before we discuss the other, shall we?"

"If you insist."

Alex stared at him. "Well, you've outlined our options rather neatly. Any ideas?"

"We could start a zoo," he offered.

"A zoo."

A bit hastily Noah said, "I was just kidding."

"Noah?"

"Yes?"

After a long moment of staring at him with unblinking eyes, Alex smiled slowly and leaned over to slide her arms around his neck. "You know," she said, "I never thought much of those ditsy ladies in the old movies who'd climb up in some man's lap and start kissing and hugging to get what they wanted. It always struck me as being rather underhanded and devious, because those guys were, of course, just putty waiting for a molding hand."

Noah cleared his throat strongly. "And so?"

"And so, I'd never try that on you. Never. It would be just terrible of me to take advantage of this violent passion you're laboring under. Just terrible. I wouldn't be able to hold my head up for the shame I'd feel. I mean, to resort to such underhanded feminine tricks would be to admit that I couldn't win a debate with you. That I couldn't converse like any sensible adult. I'd be resorting to some horrible sexist trade-off, offering my willing body in return for what I really wanted from you."

Noah cleared his throat again, his arms moving of their own volition to encircle Alex as her weight settled into his lap.

Solemnly she went on. "It'd be the most awful thing I could possibly do, cheating both of us of an opportunity to grow and learn as sensible adults. It would deprive us of the chance to realize our full potential."

"Alex—"

"Worse, we'd be setting the bars of our cage in cement. We'd wake up one day and not know how to *talk* to each other anymore! We'd address each other by silly pet names, and embarrass everyone who heard us. We'd be so ridiculous, we wouldn't be able to *stand* each other!"

Noah had to clear his throat twice. "Alex?"

"I would never allow that to happen," she insisted solemnly. "I would never demean the both of us by resorting to such tricks. It would be unfair and unladylike. Not to mention devious and under-handed. I would never consider using your violent passion for me as a weapon or a reward. I would never wait until you were weak with desire and then demand that you give in to me. I promise you, Noah!

If I want something of you, I'll ask in a rational, reasonable manner, and we'll discuss it. And if I lose out to you logically, I promise not to cry, or cling to you, or hold passion over your head as a threat. Or a promise."

"Alex?"

She was kissing his chin. "Hmmm?"

"Um . . . what, uh, what were you going to ask me?" he managed.

"Oh, nothing important." Her fingers threaded through his hair and her lips feathered along his jaw.

"You were going to ask me something."

"Hmmm? Oh, that. It was just about the zoo."

"Zoo? What zoo?" Not that he cared.

"Our zoo. All that land, fenced and everything. We can have a zoo, can't we, Noah?" She kissed him, then kissed him again.

"Zoo?" He wondered dimly if he was repeating himself.

"Uh-huh. A children's zoo. We'll find other old and gentle animals, not the least bit dangerous." She kissed him. "And children can come and pet them. Wouldn't that be terrific?"

"Terrific," he echoed hoarsely.

"You can photograph the kids hugging a lion or riding an elephant—"

"Elephant?"

"—and they'll have a picture they'll always treasure. We can charge just a small fee for admission and the pictures, and that'll feed the animals. It'll work out just wonderfully, won't it?"

"Wonderfully." Her lips were evading his, and Noah made a blind but determined attempt to capture them."

"Say yes, Noah," she murmured.

"Yes," he growled.

"You," he told her some considerable time later, "are a witch. I knew it the first moment I looked into those green eyes. There are sirens in your eyes. It just isn't fair."

Alex, wearing only one of his shirts, was sitting cross-legged at the foot of their bed with a large pad of paper in her lap. "I know where we can get an elephant cheap," she said, carefully sketching what was, at the moment, the empty lot behind Noah's building.

He placed another pillow behind his back. "You have a one-track mind."

Green eyes with a hint of Gypsy wildness in them gleamed at him. "You're pretty unswerving yourself."

"Don't look at me like that, dammit!" he chided her. "Next time I'll find myself agreeing to something even worse than a zoo!"

Alex pulled on an innocent expression that would have shamed an angel. "Noah, you *can't* say I forced you to agree to the zoo. I told you I'd never resort to silly, demeaning tricks, after all."

"Yes, you did indeed say that. Promised, in fact. And I meant to tell you how truly enjoyable it was to have a rational, reasonable discussion with you."

"Isn't it nice to be adult about these things," she agreed, deadpan.

"Certainly. I believe I was swayed to your way of thinking by the rational argument you used when you kissed me the first time. I was convinced of the validity of your arguments when you kissed me the second time. By the third kiss I was willing to believe the sun rose in the west. Then, by—"

"And I settled for a zoo?" she mourned, her eyes laughing.

"Would you please have a little respect for a man having a temper tantrum, and not interrupt?" he requested politely.

"Sorry. You were saying?"

He sighed again. "I've lost the thread, dammit."

Alex tossed the pad and pencil aside and rejoined him at the head of the bed. "Good," she said cheerfully. "Tantrums are very immature."

"This is the woman I saw throwing pillows one morning?"

"That was an entirely different kind of tantrum. Perfectly logical and reasonable."

"The hell you say."

She giggled. "Well, never mind. I'm sure you'll find some way of getting even with me for using a silly, demeaning trick."

Noah smiled slowly.

Suspicious, she eyed him. "I can see the wheels turning."

Leaning on his elbow, Noah began very methodically to unbutton her shirt. "I was just thinking," he said, placing a kiss beside each button as it was unfastened, "that sauce for the gander . . . is sauce for the goose as well."

Alex knew—she *knew*—that he was using her own methods on her, but that knowledge did absolutely nothing to keep her heart from pounding or her breath from growing short. "I refuse," she said, smothering a gasp as a kiss landed beside her navel, "to let you resort to a cheap sexist trick to get your way!"

"I'd never do that," he told her, hurt. He began pressing warm kisses in a widening path back up toward her throat.

Alex found her fingers tangled in his hair. "It would be unworthy of you. Demeaning. Unfair."

"Of course it would."

She helped him to discard the shirt. "I'd never forgive you," she said weakly, her hands seeking his muscled back.

"Of course you would."

"Brute!" she accused him breathlessly.

Between kisses he said, "There's just . . . one . . . small thing . . . I want . . . of you, Alex."

"What?" she managed.

"I agreed to your zoo," he reminded her.

"Uh-huh." She could feel her bones melting and dissolving.

"And now I want you to agree to something." He kissed her urgently.

Alex made a sound in her throat that could have been taken for a question.

"I want you to promise to say I do," he whispered, a breath away from her lips.

"I do," she said obediently, lifting her head blindly to seek that tormenting mouth.

He evaded her. "Promise to say it when it counts," he told her huskily. "Say you promise, Alex."

"I promise!"

"You should be ashamed," she told him sleepily.

Noah reached to turn out the lamp on the nightstand, chuckling. "I'm not. Are you awake?"

"Not really."

"Alex, pay attention."

She yawned and burrowed closer to his side. "Do I have to?" she asked him plaintively.

"Yes." His voice was firm. "I can't go to sleep until I'm sure you're really going to marry me."

It woke her up. Alex lifted her head and stared at him. The full moon shining through the window lit them both in a stark white light. Carefully she said, "I seem to remember agreeing to something along those lines."

His blue-gray eyes were steady and warm. "I love you, Alex," he said quietly. "So much. I'll never be able to tell you how much. This blue-ribbon affair of ours, it's always been forever to me. Tell me it's the same for you. Marry me."

Alex drew a deep, shuddering breath, unaware until that moment of just how desperately she'd needed this confirmation of his love. The girl who had never quite forgotten how it felt to be an unwanted orphanage brat wanted to cry suddenly in the joyous relief of being loved as she loved.

"Yes," she whispered. "Yes, Noah."

His face seemed alight from within. He drew her forward to kiss her tenderly, then held her in an embrace so full of love it nearly stopped her heart. Listening to his heart beating steadily beneath her cheek, she drifted toward sleep in her contentment.

"I love you," she whispered.

"I love you too. . . ."

She thought that he murmured something else, but Alex was too near sleep to be certain. Vaguely she thought she'd have to confide her ridiculous obsession that they'd lived and loved before. She still felt the grief of losing him twice, but the dreams had stopped. Did that mean something? she wondered. Probably. Her mind, eager not to lose this man, had dreamed of loss.

That had to be it.

There was really nothing else it could be.

Noah woke with a start in the small hours of the morning. Alex was held securely in his arms, and he hugged her sleeping body gently. These dreams, he thought, had been curiously final. He knew, somehow, that he wouldn't dream of a Southern lady or a Gypsy girl anymore.

All stories ended.

And he'd seen the endings of two stories tonight.

Nine

They spent another week at the cabin, both enjoying the quiet and each other's company. Cal, who had until then kept his distance from Noah, clearly regarding the man's presence in Alex's life warily, completely relaxed after the "male" confrontation concerning who would sleep in her bed.

Alex was relieved that the lion had become openly affectionate with Noah, and amused when Cal apparently decided that since Noah was the dominant male of the two, it was perfectly natural that he become a playmate equal in stature—and size.

"Noah? Are you all right?"

"I never realized," Noah wheezed, "that four hundred pounds could weigh so much. Could you get him off my chest before he caves in my rib cage, please?"

"He's only playing with you."

With some skill Noah worked his way out from under Cal's considerable weight. The lion managed a last affectionate hug that deprived his playmate of most of his remaining breath, and then let him get to his feet.

"Playing with me? He's trying to squeeze me to death!"

"You're the dominant lion," Alex reminded him, trying not to laugh. "You proved that to him. So he thinks you're bigger than he is."

"You mean I'm going to get tackled like that again? Just because I rousted him out of your bed?"

"Something like that."

"Oh, damn."

"It's your fault. You won the lioness, after all."

"I thought I won the blue ribbon."

"*We* won the blue ribbon. You won the lioness."

Noah pulled her into his arms, ignoring the lion gumming his ankle. "Oh? And what did you win?"

Alex linked her fingers together behind her neck. She was thinking of two women who had loved a man with gray-blue eyes . . . and lost him. "I won . . . more than you'll ever know," she murmured.

His eyes were alight. "Sprite, you can have ten zoos if you like. Just as long as I have you."

They might have remained at the cabin indefinitely, but both realized there could be no firm plans for their own future until Caliban's safety had been assured. That would require their return to San

Francisco, and it posed more problems than either liked to think about.

Starting a zoo on Noah's land meant having it rezoned or getting a special permit from the city, neither of which was going to be simple. There was also the matter of explaining her possession of Cal: she had no bill of sale, and had transported the animal across the country, breaking various laws in every state she'd passed through.

Cal's wasn't the only future in doubt.

She didn't mention it to Noah, but he brought the subject up himself when they were packing the van. It was late afternoon: they were timing their return trip to reach home just before dawn.

"We need a bill of sale," he said abruptly.

Alex was kneeling just inside the van, arranging boxes to leave room for the pets. She glanced through the door at Noah, then briefly beyond him to where Cal and Buddy lay sprawled a few feet away in the sunlight. "Maybe we can get by without one," she said, knowing just how impossible it would be to obtain.

Noah handed her a small box and frowned as he watched her get it into place with the others. "You know better than that. One of the first questions someone's going to ask is where we got Cal. We'll have to get a vet to look at him too: they'll require a health certificate." He studied her averted face for a moment. "Is there any chance at all of getting a bill of sale? The circus owner—"

She was shaking her head. "The circus disbanded

a couple of years ago, and all the animals were sold. I heard on the grapevine that the owner headed immediately for Europe. I believe he had tax problems."

"Grapevine?"

"Circus grapevine. Just because I no longer worked in one doesn't mean I've lost interest in the circus. Whenever one came into town, I visited. And circus people are always friendly to one of their own."

"How friendly?" he asked slowly.

Alex sat back on her heels and stared at him. "You have something in mind?"

"Maybe." Noah sat just inside the van. He smiled crookedly. "Since we've already broken the law— several laws, in fact—I'm not about to balk at breaking another if it'll ensure Cal's future. How about you?"

Very dryly she said, "I'm facing a few stiff fines and a possible jail term; what's one more broken law?"

"A very small broken law," Noah said absently, frowning in obvious thought. "And we wouldn't be the only ones breaking it. That—to coin a phrase—is the rub. Whether it works will depend on just how friendly circus people are to their own. Would a circus person who was a stranger to you be willing to help us save Cal?"

She saw where he was heading. "You mean would one of them fake a bill of sale?"

"What d'you think?"

"If," Alex said slowly, "it was a small circus, someone might. It depends. Circus people are individuals—some have more scruples than others."

Noah smiled at that remark. Then he got to his feet. "Well, it's the only out I can see. Without a bill of sale we're sunk. With one at least we'll be standing on partially legal ground." He reached for the last box. "So tell me—how do we find a circus between here and San Francisco?"

Alex took the box and placed it with the others, smiling. "We find a phone," she said briskly.

"Whom do we call?" he asked in a rueful tone.

"A lady I know. She was a circus performer back when it really *meant* something; she keeps up with the whereabouts of every circus in existence."

"Is that possible?"

"It is for her. Every circus, from Ringling Brothers on down, keeps her on their mailing list. She has schedules and programs that are up-to-date, and lots of people write to tell her the latest gossip. Believe me, she'll know where the nearest circus is."

They had to take a chance and leave the cabin earlier than planned. Both were uneasy over the prospect of hauling a lion around in a van for as much as a couple of days, depending on where the nearest circus could be found, but they had little choice. They could hardly leave the pets alone in the cabin.

They found a phone as quickly as possible since the lady Alex meant to call lived in the Midwest—another time zone. The phone was at a small convenience store off the beaten path, and Noah pulled the van close; he remained inside and kept a wary eye on passersby. And he listened with interest to Alex's side of the conversation: he could hear her easily since she'd left the booth's door open.

"Sassy? Hi, it's Alex. I know I promised to call, but things have been a little crazy. Yes, I moved to San Francisco, and that's part of the reason I'm calling now. I want to settle there permanently. Well, I have a small problem. You remember Caliban? Oh, he's fine, but I have to make him legal. I need someone to write up a bill of sale. Yes. A circus, I thought. Somewhere near San Francisco."

Noah watched her face as she listened intently, and saw it brighten.

"It's in Stockton? Didn't Carlos sign up with Cordova? I thought so. That's perfect, Sassy! He owes me. That time in Kansas City, you remember? He should be all healed by now." Alex laughed suddenly. "I'll remind him! And I'll be calling you soon, Sassy. Yes. Thanks a lot. 'Bye."

Noah waited until she'd returned to the passenger seat. "I gather this lady knows about Cal?"

"She's one of the few people who does."

"And who is Carlos?" he asked politely.

Alex was smiling, her eyes bright. "Someone who owes me a favor," she said, clearly relishing the thought. "Head for Stockton: the Cordova circus is in town."

Pulling the van out onto the highway, Noah sent her a glance. "Not to belabor a point, but why does he owe you a favor?"

"I pulled a Bengal tiger off him," Alex said calmly.

After a moment, when he could trust his voice, Noah said, "I see. I gather he was in the process of getting hurt?"

"Mauled is more like it. That tiger hated men, and Carlos didn't believe me when I told him that. He went into the cage before I could stop him. There wasn't time to go for the tranquilizer gun, so I had to go in after him."

"And you pulled the tiger off him—with your bare hands?"

"Seemed the thing to do at the time."

Noah shook his head. "My darling sprite, if you ever do something like that around me, I'll lock you up. If I don't die of heart failure first."

"It was my job, Noah, and I knew what I was doing." Avoiding an argument, she went on hastily. "The point is, Carlos said he'd do anything he could to repay me. And he has a true Latin tongue; if he can't talk Cordova into providing us with a bill of sale, I don't know him."

"But you do know him," Noah said.

Alex looked at him in surprise. "If I didn't know *you* better, I could swear . . ."

"That I was jealous?" He smiled just a little. "I am."

"Why?" she asked blankly. "Noah, you surely can't doubt how I feel about you! I love you. Carlos was never more than a friend, and sometimes not even that."

After a moment Noah spoke slowly. "It isn't that. I'm not jealous of him the way I'd be of another man in your past. It's just—he's a part of that world you belonged to. He knows the people you know, knows a way of life that's familiar to you. D'you understand, Alex? He knows a part of *you* I wish I could have known."

She watched his serious profile and listened, beginning to understand, finally, the yearning look in his eyes whenever he'd asked her about her life in the circus.

"You were a child when you ran away to the circus, and you grew to be a woman there. I think that's something a man always wishes he could have known about the woman he loves. And for us, that part of your life is so damned important. You didn't just grow up, you learned a whole new set of instincts, a completely different way of life. I wish I could have seen that, Alex."

Alex didn't quite know what to say, but an instinctive part of her found words. "That coming of age wasn't very important to the people I lived with then, Noah. It wasn't unusual to them, so they didn't watch. They didn't care." She leaned across the console to touch his cheek briefly. "And Carlos wouldn't have seen it anyway. He was with our circus for only a few months before he moved on, and that was just before I left myself. He was a trainer between jobs, traveling."

Noah nodded and sent her a smile. "I just wanted you to understand how I feel about that part of your life," he said huskily.

In a quiet voice she said, "You came of age in a war."

"Yes."

"I'd never want to see a war," she said. "But I wish I could have seen a boy become a man. I wish I could have seen that part of you." She could remember blue-gray eyes that were weary, devastated by war, and she wished she could have held Noah at that moment in his life the way she had held that other soldier, and perhaps eased his pain.

Noah reached out for her hand, holding it tightly. After a long moment he said softly, "There were times then that I dreamed about someone like you. Those dreams kept me sane."

Alex lifted his hand to her cheek, silent, wondering about that other soldier. Had he died in that war despite a woman's conviction that he lived? Was that why he hadn't come back to her? She pushed the thoughts away, grateful that this man had survived a war to find her.

They stopped briefly to buy take-out food along the way, then halted and parked the van some distance off the little-traveled road to catch a few hours sleep; they wanted to arrive in Stockton early in the morning. The pets were fed and allowed to stretch their legs, then all settled down to sleep.

And Alex dreamed of a blond woman laboring alone in childbirth, and of a Gypsy girl who no longer danced and sang before a campfire. . . .

*   *   *

The van was moving again when Alex woke, yawning, to find that Noah had stopped somewhere and gotten coffee and sweet rolls for breakfast.

"And you shaved," she observed, studying his smooth cheeks as she unwrapped a roll.

"I refuse to meet even a small part of your past with a morning stubble," he said calmly. "Battery-powered razors are terrific. I also let Cal stretch his legs before we started, and fed both pets. Cal ate a dozen jars of baby food, and three cans of liver."

"He doesn't eat heavily when we're traveling."

He glanced at her suddenly, quizzical. "What were you dreaming?"

"Did I say something?" she asked casually.

"No. You just looked sad."

Alex reached across him to place his coffee in the holder clipped to the window, then handed him a roll. "Aren't dreams peculiar?" she asked. "Sometimes you can't even remember them." She uncapped her own cup and placed it in the holder clipped on her side before beginning to eat her roll.

If Noah noticed that her response was evasive, he didn't comment on the fact. He ate his breakfast.

They rolled into Stockton when the sun was still low in the eastern sky, and a few questions at a service station sent them to the outskirts of town and the fields leased by the Cordova Circus.

There were tents and wagons spread around, and the air was already ringing with busy sounds. Roustabouts were working to erect the big show tent, their mallets pounding stakes into the ground, and people scurried around with buckets and equipment as wild animals greeted the morning with their own particular voices.

Noah pulled the van beneath a large tree at the edge of the field, and no one paid any attention to them. And a glance toward the interior of the van told him that Cal remained undisturbed by the nearby roars of various of his feline kin.

"I hope," Noah said, "we can leave the pets alone for a little while. I want to see this circus."

Alex knew very well that it wasn't the circus he was most interested in, but she said nothing about that. "I don't see why not. No one's likely to bother the van, and we won't be gone that long anyway. At least I hope we won't."

They locked up the van and made their way across the field. Moving through the confusion of busy people, they garnered a few curious glances, but no one stopped or questioned them.

"Do we look like circus people?" Noah asked her wryly.

"It's all in the attitude," she told him. "If you act as if you belong in a place, you can generally get away with it."

"Hi, Alex!"

"Hello, Tino."

Noah looked back as they continued walking. "Who was that?"

"A flyer. I know quite a few of these people, Noah." She was lifting a hand in acknowledgment to several other calls. "Noah?" Backtracking, she found him watching an elephant being washed, and took him by the arm. "This way."

"Did you say we could get an elephant cheap?"

"They're fascinating, aren't they?"

"I wish I had my camera." He realized they were taking what was obviously a direct route to somewhere. "D'you know where we're going?"

"Of course. Carlos is a trainer. He trains the big cats. So that's where we're going. I'm following my ears."

"I wondered."

They continued walking, occasionally dodging busy people. The sounds of restless cats were getting louder.

"Alex? Alex!"

A dark-haired man erupted through the flap of a tent, catching Alex in a hug that lifted her off the ground as he swung her in a circle.

Noah, watching silently, studied the man. He was just slightly over medium height and build except for the obviously powerful strength of his shoulders and arms. A T-shirt advertised rippling muscles—and the beginning of an ugly scar near the base of his neck. Somewhere in his late twenties or early thirties, he was quite handsome and seemed delighted to see Alex again.

Once she was set back down on her feet, Alex turned and introduced the two men, and Noah found his speculation had been correct. This was Carlos. Cheerful dark eyes filled with easy confidence met his own, and it was more than instinct that told Noah this man had been "never more than a friend" by Alex's choice alone.

The other man's lips twisted oddly as they shook hands, but he was smiling casually when he returned his attention to Alex.

"Still circus, Alex?" he asked.

"No, not anymore, Carlos. Not for years. But we're planning to start a children's zoo in San Francisco, and I need a favor."

"Name it," he said promptly.

"Don't agree so quickly," she said. "I'll be asking you to sink your scruples."

"Scruples? You saved my life, *cara*; what use would scruples be to a dead man? Ask away."

Alex seemed faintly surprised as she gazed at him, but shrugged as though to herself and asked. "I need a bill of sale for an adult male lion. You remember Cal?"

"The toothless kitten? Is he still alive?"

"Very much so." Alex grinned a little. "I stole him. Now I need to make him legal so he can be a part of our zoo. Can you help me?"

"I gather this is a rush job?" He didn't seem the least bit surprised by the request.

"Very much so," Noah said.

Carlos looked at him, and for a moment there was something very like an instinctive challenge in his dark eyes. Then the hot flicker was gone, and he was smiling again. Almost ruefully. "Sorry," he said directly to Noah. "I spend too much time in cages. I sometimes forget the law of the jungle doesn't hold true outside the bars."

"Maybe it does," Noah said pleasantly.

The dark eyes weighed him, then flicked toward Alex's puzzled face. "Yes," he said dryly. "Maybe it does. Give me a few minutes, Alex, and I'll see what I can do." He strode off toward the line of wagons nearby.

"What," Alex asked, "was that all about?"

Noah smiled down at her, feeling for the first time that he really had won a lioness. "What was what all about?" he repeated.

"For a minute there I thought it was going to be bared bodkins at twenty paces," she said, bewildered. "Like two lions about to lunge at each other's throats. I told you Carlos was only a friend."

"Takes two lions to lunge," he reminded her pointedly.

She looked confused for a moment, then frowned at him. "Carlos never even made a pass, for heaven's sake!"

Noah took her arm and led her back the way they'd come. "Let's go see the elephants being washed," he said brightly, "while we wait for Carlos to come back."

Alex knew a change of subject when she heard one. She accepted this one, deciding not to probe—right now, anyway—into what looked like another of those purely male matters.

But she wondered.

Carlos's few minutes stretched into an hour, but neither Noah nor Alex minded. They wandered

around, Alex introducing him to various old friends
and explaining how a circus was set up. A vendor not
yet set up for the coming night and expected crowds
nonetheless supplied them with soft drinks and
peanuts.

And Noah had to restrain Alex firmly when she
spotted yet another old friend. In a cage.

"But that's Simba!"

"Alex, please. I know I said that I wanted to see this
part of your life, but I *don't* want to see you in a cage
with a tiger!"

"He wouldn't hurt her," Carlos said, appearing
suddenly beside him. "She raised him."

In spite of Noah's cautious grip on her arm, Alex
had leaned forward to reach through the bars of a
cage and was rubbing a fierce-looking tiger behind
his left ear. The beast was nearly purring. Then she
straightened and looked hopefully at Carlos. "Any
luck?"

With a flourish Carlos produced a paper and
presented it to her. "But of course. Cordova's a friend
of mine—in addition to being my boss."

"I thought she was," Alex said with a lift of one
brow before turning her attention to the bill of sale.

Noah was watching Carlos. He saw a flicker of some
emotion cross the other man's face as he gazed on
Alex's downbent head, but it was gone too quickly to
be defined. By sight. Noah thought he could identify
it by instinct.

Regret. Perhaps loss.

Then Carlos was speaking casually. "If anyone

asks, the Cordova Circus sold you an old male lion. Actually we had to have an old one destroyed a few days ago, so it fits pretty well. The bill's dated for today; sale price cheap but believable. Anyone here'll back up the story. And now," he finished, "I owe Elena."

Alex looked up, her face glowing. "Well, you don't owe me anymore. We're even, Carlos. Thank you so much!"

Carlos reached out to brush his knuckles briefly against her cheek. "Not quite, *cara*. I haven't forgotten Simba's teeth in my back."

Noah sent a glance toward the placid tiger. "Him?"

"Him," Carlos confirmed. "He still doesn't like men, but I never turn my back to him. A lesson I learned the hard way."

"I still consider us even," Alex said firmly, holding out her hand.

Carlos shook hands with her and then with Noah, and his eyes met the other man's obliquely. "You've got quite a lady here, friend," he said almost roughly. "Take care of her."

"Always," Noah told him, quiet.

Alex stared after the retreating man, her expression startled. "How strange," she murmured. "I haven't seen him in more than six years. But for a minute there I thought . . . Well, never mind. Let's go, okay?"

Noah fell into step beside her silently. He didn't agree completely with Alex. It wasn't, he thought, strange at all. Six months . . . six years . . . six centuries. A woman like Alex could haunt a man for a very long time. But Noah agreed with her unfinished comment.

For a minute there he, too, had thought Carlos was going to cry.

"You said he wasn't always a friend," Noah said as they left the circus behind. "What did you mean?"

She shrugged. "Just that. When we first met, we got along like two cats tied up in a bag. Clash of personalities, I guess. Gradually, though, we started to talk and . . . things changed. It's funny, though . . ."

"What?"

"I never felt quite at ease around Carlos," she confessed, faintly bewildered. "He was never one of the shady characters I had to be on guard around, but . . . Oh, I don't know."

"Maybe he wanted something you couldn't give him."

Alex stared at Noah for a moment, then laughed a bit uncertainly. "I told you, he never even made a pass."

Noah was silent, then reached to take her hand. "He's a trainer, too, Alex. He wouldn't have to make a pass to realize you weren't interested, I think."

"You're imaginging things," she scoffed.

He squeezed her hand. "Am I? I suppose."

After a few miles had passed behind them, Alex said suddenly, "Was that why you two looked at each other like that? As if . . ."

"As if we both wanted the lioness?"

"Good Lord," she said blankly.

Noah chuckled softly.

Even with several stops along the way to purposely kill time, it was barely dusk when the van pulled up in front of their building in San Francisco. Neither of them wanted to tempt fate by letting Cal go public a moment sooner than necessary; even though they now had a bill of sale, some tricky footwork lay ahead of them if they weren't to be fined, jailed, or both, for the illegal possession of a wild animal.

Both Noah and Alex got out of the van to prowl the grounds all around the building as well as inside before letting the lion out. They checked and double-checked, then hurried Cal inside to relative safety.

They thought.

Ten

It had been a very long day with only a few hours sleep snatched the night before, and they were tired. They had also momentarily underestimated the diligence of the local animal control office. Or perhaps it was simply that they felt safer than ever before and relaxed their guard.

So they left the door to Alex's loft open while they transferred boxes and bags inside, content in the knowledge that both pets were happily eating supper in the kitchen.

It wasn't their fault that Teddy had decided to work nights.

Alex froze when she straightened from placing a box near the partition that was hiding her lion from shrewd brown eyes. She knew the lion was hidden for the moment, but even toothless lions make some noise when eating.

"Hello, Teddy," she said weakly.

The other woman leaned against the doorjamb and smiled easily, giving Noah a friendly nod when he hurried from the bedroom where he'd just deposited Alex's suitcase. "Hi, you two. Have a nice vacation? Oh, the door was open. Hope you don't mind?"

"Not at all," Noah said hollowly.

Alex didn't have to look at his face to realize they both wore perfect waxworks expressions of horror. Telltale sounds came from behind the partition, and they didn't stop when a small white kitten came around to climb up Alex's leg. She detached tiny claws from her jeans automatically, lifting Buddy so that he could balance easily on the back of the couch.

"What a cute kitten!" Teddy said cheerfully, coming farther into the loft.

"Isn't he? He just wandered in one day," Alex said.

Teddy stroked the kitten, still smiling at Alex. She nodded toward the kitchen. "Quite an appetite, from the sound of it. I didn't know you had a dog."

After a moment Alex sat down on the arm of the couch. She looked up at Noah as he came to stand by her side, then returned her gaze to Teddy. "I don't have a dog," she said on a sigh.

"No, I didn't think so. You have a lion, don't you, Alex?"

Alex nodded slowly, her eyes still locked with those shrewd brown ones. Which way would Teddy jump? She didn't know. "Yes. Yes, I have a lion."

Cal wandered around the partition just then. He blinked large golden eyes at Teddy, then sat down and began rubbing an itching ear against Noah's hip.

"I have a very old lion," Alex said quietly. "A very gentle and loving lion." She felt Noah's hand warmly rest on her shoulder and was more than grateful for his silent support. "A lion who's never in his life hurt a living thing."

"Where'd you get him?"

Alex didn't hesitate. "I stole him from a circus six years ago. He'd lost all his teeth, and they were going to destroy him."

"You've kept him hidden for six years?"

"Yes." Alex looked up at Noah again, smiling because she loved him so much, her heart turning over at his instant tender smile. Then she looked back at Teddy. "When anyone got too close before, I ran. I couldn't run this time."

Bright eyes glanced from one to the other of them, then briefly studied the lion. "I see. Were you planning to go on hiding him?"

"No." Alex shook her head. "A circus friend of mine faked a bill of sale for us. We're hoping to start a children's zoo. Old, gentle animals that kids can pet. If we can get the permits."

Teddy watched as the lion came to sprawl nearly at her feet, and she smiled a little when the white kitten leaped off the couch to land on a broad, patient head and began to chew on a round ear.

"He seems gentle enough. How old is he?"

"Thirty-one."

The other woman's face went still as she looked at Alex, sympathy stirring in her brown eyes. "Then he is . . . very old."

"Yes."

After an eternally long moment Teddy nodded as if to herself. "I have a few friends downtown," she said briskly. "I think maybe we can get those permits for you." Her eyes gleamed at Noah. "You may have trouble renting these lofts, but I'll take one."

"You've got it," Noah said. "Rent free."

"Oh, no." Teddy chuckled softly. "That'd be considered bribing an officer—or something like that. No, I'll pay rent, Noah. It'll be well worth the price of admission to watch you cope with a zoo!" She laughed again. "I'll start the wheels turning downtown tomorrow. For now I'll leave you two to your unpacking." She turned for the door.

"Teddy?" Alex knew her cheeks were wet, and didn't give a damn.

"Yes?"

"Thank you."

"Don't thank me, Alex." She smiled widely. "I'm a sucker for old lions, white kittens . . . and love. See you." And she was gone, closing the door quietly behind her.

Alex found herself held tightly in Noah's arms, laughing and crying at once. Relief and happiness were filling her until she thought she'd burst.

"You startled hell out of me by telling her the truth," Noah said, leading her around so that they could sit on the couch. "But I decided you knew what you were doing."

"Did you?" Alex wiped her cheeks with the back of her hand and grinned at him. "I didn't. I just hoped Teddy would be with us rather than against us, crossed my fingers, and jumped."

"You took quite a chance."

Alex leaned against him with a sigh. "I know, but somehow I just had a feeling she wouldn't take Cal away." With a frown she added, "And *why* do I think she should be taller every time I see her?"

"That's odd, I keep thinking the same thing."

For a crazy moment Alex wondered if Teddy had played a part in their past lives. A helpful part, maybe? Then she winced. It was tangled enough *now*!

"Since we have Cal's future settled," Noah said, smiling at her, "shall we make firm plans for our own?"

Alex decided the time had come. She wouldn't feel comfortable in keeping her dreams from Noah, not when they had influenced her so much. "Um, Noah, there's something I want to tell you about."

"If it's a bar to matrimony, I don't want to hear about it," he said definitely.

"No, nothing like that. At least—it certainly hasn't changed my mind, although it might change yours."

"Nothing could change my mind."

Alex rose to her feet and began to wander around the room aimlessly, trying to find words for the impossible. "Ever since we met, I've been having . . . dreams."

"Dreams?"

He sounded startled, she thought, and her pacing became even more aimless. "Yes. Odd dreams. At first I didn't really think much about them. Or at least I didn't *want* to think about them. They seemed to be—were—pieces of two stories, two lives. And each story progressed very neatly and logically, with beginnings and middles . . . and endings.

"One story was about a Gypsy girl and a lord's son. And the other was about a union soldier and a Southern lady. But somehow I *knew* that *I* was the Gypsy girl and the Southern lady, and that *you* were the lord's son and the union soldier."

"Alex—"

She interrupted him, hurrying on. "When I began believing that what I dreamed were actually memories of past lives, I started to worry that you and I were caught up in some strange pattern of—oh, hell—fate, for want of a better word. Because those endings I dreamed weren't happy ones. I lost you. The Gypsy girl was sent away, and the union soldier rode back into the war—"

"I came back to you, Alex."

Alex felt a shock that was oddly both hot and cold, his husky words and the meaning behind them stopping the breath in her throat and halting her restless steps. "You—?"

"I came back to you."

She turned slowly to stare at him.

He was on his feet only a few steps away. "That soldier," he said softly, "came back to the beautiful Southern lady, and the child that was theirs."

She hadn't told him about the child, Alex realized wildly. How could he have known? Unless . . .

"I've been dreaming too."

Alex swallowed hard. "And the Gypsy girl? You sent her away."

"No. My father sent her away. Paid her brothers gold to take her away. But I found you, Alex."

The certainty in his voice was too strong to be questioned. And Alex didn't want to question. It felt too right; they were both too certain to be wrong.

She stepped toward him and held out her right hand. "Look at the lifeline," she said softly.

He took her hand, studying for a moment, then looked at his own palm. She traced her lifeline and his with her left index finger.

"From this point—the point where we met—our lifelines match. It's impossible, but they match."

"Fated to share all our lives together," he concluded, lifting shimmering silver eyes to hers.

Alex drew a shaken breath. "I'm not sure that I believe in any of this."

"It's probably something much simpler," he agreed. "Like telepathy."

She looked down at their palms. "Just lines on skin," she observed.

"Just lines. Not, after all, much else. Lines."

"Reincarnation . . . there's no way to prove it."

He nodded. "No way to *know*. Just faith. Belief."

They stared at each other.

"I love you," he said. "I've always loved you. I loved you when you danced in front of a campfire, and when you hid me from soldiers. You taught me what love meant in a clearing near a stream, and in a bedroom with an old rock fireplace. Leaving you to go back to a war was the hardest thing I've ever had to do, and finding you after my father's cruelty was finding a heaven I thought I'd lost."

It held the sound of vows spoken from the heart, and Alex's heart responded instantly.

"I love you. I loved you when you were a union soldier and when I was a Gypsy girl. I loved you when you went away to war, and even when I thought you'd paid to be rid of me. I've been searching for you, searching for someone I couldn't name. And when I found you this time I was so desperately afraid of losing you."

Noah enfolded her in his arms, holding her tightly. "Marry me," he whispered.

"Yes." Alex slipped her arms around his neck as he lifted her and strode toward the bedroom. "Yes, my love."

It wasn't the same little glade, but the Gypsy girl was drawn to it because it reminded her of that other one. She sat on a fallen log and stared at the stream, memories tormenting her. Months. Months, and they were far from the place where she'd learned of love . . . and betrayal. The gold was long since spent, her brothers' jeering triumph lessened by time.

Her own pain was an ache even time could not heal.

She felt more than heard someone coming, but stared at the stream blindly. No. It wasn't he. It was never he. But she heard a soft sound and looked up despite herself, everything in her going still. This time it was he.

"They lied," he said hoarsely, looking at her with desperate need. "They lied to you. My sweet, don't say their lies have killed your love. Don't say it's too late for us!"

With a wild cry she flew to his embrace, the coldness gone forever. She listened to his broken endearments, to the sound of his heart pounding in time with hers, and her own murmurs of love were the outpourings of a heart filled with a fierce, joyous release. . . .

She no longer stared down the dusty, empty road, but a part of her could not help glancing from time to time. And today was a hot and sunny day, much as that day had been. On this day, though, her son played happily on a blanket spread beneath the big oak tree, his infant gurgles mingling with the sounds of birds in the branches high above him.

She sat nearby, her fingers occupied with the mending in her lap and her mind ranging free. Memories. She hoarded them within her heart. Her fingers moved automatically as she lifted her head and sent a yearning glance down the dusty road. Then her fingers stilled.

The mending fell at her feet as she rose, heart pounding. A horse was coming down the road. A single horse and rider. She walked toward the gate steadily, hope and dread clashing within her, biting her lip to hold back the cry of desperate longing. It would be just a stranger, asking for a dipper of water or a meal or directions. Just another stranger to pass through her life briefly. So briefly.

But . . . dear God, he looked familiar! Straight and broad-shouldered in the saddle. No uniform, of course, but the hot sun shone down on golden hair.

Her heart stopped, then began thudding against her ribs.

It was he!

She waited, still and silent, by the gate. Stared into blue-gray eyes as he swung from the horse and stepped toward her. And when he held out his arms, she went into them with no more than a sigh.

"I love you," he said huskily, fiercely. "I've nothing to offer you, but—"

"That's enough," she whispered, gazing up at him tenderly. "It's more than enough."

He framed her face in warm hands, eyes alight, and kissed her with aching gentleness. Then his eyes were drawn by the sounds of a child, and he looked back at her with incredulous hope.

Smiling, she took his hand and led him toward the blanket beneath the big oak tree. "Come and meet your son, my love."

And he held a babe with blue-gray eyes. . . .

Alex smiled and listened to the heart beating steadily beneath her cheek.

All stories had endings.

And some endings . . . were no more than beginnings.

THE EDITOR'S CORNER

As you know from the sneak previews I've been giving in the Editor's Corner, you have some wonderful treats in store—and none better than the four for next month!

We start off with a gloriously intense and touching love story in **CHAR'S WEBB,** LOVESWEPT #151, by Kathleen Downes. The story begins on an astonishing note: Hero Keith Webb has "invented" a fiancée because the young daughter of a friend has a crush on him and he wants to let her down gently. For his lady love he had chosen a first name he'd always liked, Charlotte, and for her last—well, his imagination failed and he had only come up with Smith. Now, just put yourself in Keith's place when the management consulting firm he hired sends out one of their best and brightest employees and *she* introduces herself as—you guessed it!—Charlotte Smith. The real Charlotte is as lovely, sensitive, and tender-hearted as Keith's fantasy fiancée . . . but she's also devoted to her job, has vowed never to mix work and love and—ah, but to say more would give away too much of a vastly entertaining and twisty plot, so I'll only encourage you to anticipate being trapped like Keith in the enchantment of **CHAR'S WEBB.**

If you've just finished **ALWAYS,** my guess is that you feel as though you've been wrung out emotionally. (I certainly felt that way when I read and worked on that marvelous love story!) Now, for next month, Iris Johansen greatly changes pace with **EVERLASTING,** LOVESWEPT #152, in which she gives you a romp of a romance. Oh, it is intensely emotional, too, of course, but it *is* also a true "Johansen romp." You met Kira Rubinoff in **ALWAYS** and may have leaped to the correct conclusion that she was your next heroine. In **EVERLASTING** she is off to America for help to rescue her beloved Marna . . . and

continued

that help is in the form of one Zack Damon, powerful industrialist, famed lover, part American Indian and proud of his heritage—in short, just one heck of a hero. Now for the romp part: there are gypsies and dungeons, palaces, plots, magic, and kings. And there is grand, glorious, passionate romantic love between Kira and Zack. Iris simply keeps coming up with one lovely romance after another, and aren't we lucky?

Our other two authors for the month—the much loved Miz Pickart and Miz Brown—have just as wonderful and fertile imaginations. First, you'll enjoy Joan's charming **MISTER LONELYHEARTS,** LOVESWEPT #153. The title refers to the hero's occupation: he writes a newspaper advice column, focusing primarily on love and romance. Heroine Chapel Barclay is a lawyer—and a lady who is as mad as a wet hen at the "Dear Ben" column and the blasted man who writes it! She thinks the advice he gives out is garbage, pure and simple, that it's destructive to creating real and lasting relationships. When they confront one another on a television talk show, Ben is the overwhelming winner of their debate . . . and later full of remorse that the lovely Chapel had suffered from his remarks, even though he'd softened them because of her remarkable effect on him. But if Ben and Chapel had thought sparks had flown between them on that telecast, did they have a surprise ahead. When he sought her out to apologize, it was the beginning of a physical and emotional conflagration that made the great Chicago blaze look like a small campfire! Another memorable winner from Joan Elliott Pickart.

Sandra Brown's stunningly beautiful contribution to your reading enjoyment next month is **22 INDIGO PLACE,** LOVESWEPT #154. A romance of conflict and drama and sensuality, **22 INDIGO PLACE** is aptly titled, since the house at this address has played such an important role throughout the lives of the heroine and hero that it

continued

almost becomes a living, vivid character in the story. And the story of James Paden and Laura Nolan is breathtaking. James was the high school "bad boy"—complete with motorcycle, black leather jacket, and shades. Laura was "Miss Goody Two-Shoes." Their contacts back then were brief yet fierce, and when they meet again their impact on one another is just as dramatic. But now, added to James's devastating sensual power over Laura, is his economic power. How he wields it and witholds it makes for one of Sandra Brown's best ever love stories.

We hope you enjoy these four LOVESWEPTs as much as everyone here in the office did.

Warm good wishes,

Sincerely,

Carolyn Nichols

Carolyn Nichols
  Editor
LOVESWEPT
Bantam Books, Inc.
666 Fifth Avenue
New York, NY 10103

LOVESWEPT

Love Stories you'll never forget by authors you'll always remember

☐	21753	**Stubborn Cinderalla #135** Eugenia Riley	$2.50
☐	21746	**The Rana Look #136** Sandra Brown	$2.50
☐	21750	**Tarnished Armor #137** Peggy Webb	$2.50
☐	21757	**The Eagle Catcher #138** Joan Elliott Pickart	$2.50
☐	21755	**Delilah's Weakness #139** Kathleen Creighton	$2.50
☐	21758	**Fire In The Rain #140** Fayrene Preston	$2.50
☐	21759	**Crescendo #141** A. Staff & S. Goldenbaum	$2.50
☐	21754	**Trouble In Triplicate #142** Barbara Boswell	$2.50

Prices and availability subject to change without notice.

Buy them at your local bookstore or use this handy coupon for ordering:

LOVESWEPT

Love Stories you'll never forget by authors you'll always remember

☐	21760	**Donovan's Angel #143** Peggy Webb	$2.50
☐	21761	**Wild Blue Yonder #144** Millie Grey	$2.50
☐	21762	**All Is Fair . . . #145** Linda Cajio	$2.50
☐	21763	**Journey's End #146** Joan Elliott Pickart	$2.50
☐	21751	**Once In Love With Amy #147** Nancy Holder	$2.50
☐	21749	**Always #148** Iris Johansen	$2.50
☐	21765	**Time After Time #149** Kay Hooper	$2.50
☐	21767	**Hot Tamales #150** Sara Orwig	$2.50

Prices and availability subject to change without notice.

Buy them at your local bookstore or use this handy coupon for ordering:

Bantam Books, Inc., Dept. SW3, 414 East Golf Road, Des Plaines, Ill. 60016

Please send me the books I have checked above. I am enclosing $_____
(please add $1.50 to cover postage and handling). Send check or money order
—no cash or C.O.D.'s please.

Mr/Mrs/Miss _____

Address_____

City _____ State/Zip_____

SW3—7/86

Please allow four to six weeks for delivery. This offer expires 1/87.

Special Offer
Buy a Bantam Book
for only 50¢.

Now you can have an up-to-date listing of Bantam's hundreds of titles plus take advantage of our unique and exciting bonus book offer. A special offer which gives you the opportunity to purchase a Bantam book for only 50¢. Here's how!

By ordering any five books at the regular price per order, you can also choose any other single book listed (up to a $4.95 value) for just 50¢. Some restrictions do apply, but for further details why not send for Bantam's listing of titles today!

Just send us your name and address and we will send you a catalog!

BANTAM BOOKS, INC.
P.O. Box 1006, South Holland, Ill. 60473

Mr. Mrs. Miss Ms. _____
　　　　　　　　　　　　　(please print)

Address _____

City _____ State _____ Zip _____

FC(A)—11/85

Please allow four to six weeks for delivery. This offer expires 5 86.